Sign
of the Spirit

Kay Cornelius

Frontiers of Faith Series: Book Four

Heartsong Presents

Dedication

To my pastor, John Dees, and the members of Willowbrook
Baptist Church, particularly the women of the J.O.Y. and
Faith Sunday school classes, who have been generous in
their support, encouragement, and prayers.

Acknowledgement

Thanks to Tammy Owen and Mike Balazsy of Madison Books
and Computers for their ever-cheerful assistance and pa-
tience in helping me through the maze of computer tech-
nology.

*But the Spirit maketh intercession for us
with groanings which cannot be uttered.* —Romans 8:26

A note from the Author:
*I love to hear from my readers! You may write to me at
the following address:* **Kay Cornelius
Author Relations
P.O. Box 719
Uhrichsville, OH 44683**

ISBN 1-55748-700-6

SIGN OF THE SPIRIT

Cover illustration by Kathy Arbuckle.

PRINTED IN THE U.S.A.

one

Kentucky, 1782

Although it was mid-afternoon and the warmest part of the day, the October sun shone so feebly that Susannah McKay Campbell drew her woolen shawl closer around her and shivered.

"We ought to be going now," her cousin Hannah McIntyre said gently. A cold wind tugged at Hannah's bonnet, lifting its edges to reveal her fiery red hair.

"I know," Susannah said, but she made no move to step down from the doorstone of the cabin that had been her home for the precious, too-few months that she and James had lived in Kentucky.

If she didn't look behind her, Susannah could imagine that nothing had changed. Before her lay the land that James had cleared through back-breaking labor so he could build their cabin atop the highest point on the property. Every tree and canebrake that could provide a hiding place had been cleared away from around the house so that the Indians who still occasionally crossed the Ohio River to raid into Kentucky county would find no cover in which to hide and take them by surprise.

But all his hard work hadn't prevented the Indians from stealing their livestock, nor had it kept them from killing James when he went alone to seek his cattle.

"At least Indian summer seems to be at an end," Hannah said. She took Susannah's arm and stepped off the doorstone, and reluctantly Susannah followed.

"Aye," Susannah said with a trace of bitterness. "Another

5

week and we'd have been safe for the winter, and James would be with me in the spring—"

Susannah broke off, unable to continue, but Hannah knew what Susannah would have said and put a strong arm around her. By spring planting time, the long-awaited child Susannah carried should be almost six months old. After several years of marriage, she and James had almost resigned themselves to being childless. Although they never spoke of it, the sadness was always there, especially when they were with Susannah's relatives, where there was nearly always a new baby to pass around and admire. It only added to her pain that Susannah hadn't known that she carried his child until a few weeks after her husband's death.

"You must be strong now for the sake of your child," Hannah said, aware that her words were poor comfort.

"James worked so hard," Susannah said, almost to herself. "He deserved better than to die like an animal, with no chance to defend himself." Her gesture took in the bare landscape before them, bordered by a split-rail fence. "He'd never lived on the land before, yet look how much he managed to accomplish."

"Yes, James did a good job," Hannah agreed. "We were all surprised by how well he took to it. Only a few weeks ago he told Nate that his only regret was that you hadn't come to Kentucky sooner."

Susannah stared out over the land again without really seeing it, recalling with sorrow the reason behind her husband's decision to leave their North Carolina home. "I know being called a traitor hurt James far more than he let anyone know. The way he was treated in Carolina wasn't fair."

Hannah nodded in silent agreement. James Campbell's father had been a minor British official, and in the early days of the Revolution, James had joined a Loyalist Regiment of former Scots Highlanders. After they were defeated in their first and only action, James never again wore his battle tartan. But neither did he join the North Carolina Continental Line or the state militia, where the men in Susannah's family had fought. As a result, James and Susannah had been labeled Tories, and James's mercantile business in Salisbury had failed for lack of custom.

"No one here in Kentucky ever called James a Tory," Hannah said after a brief silence. "At least you have the satisfaction of knowing that he was completely happy here."

Susannah compressed her lips and sighed heavily. "So was I until now."

That's not entirely true, Hannah thought. James and Susannah had traveled to Kentucky with Hannah and her new husband, Nate McIntyre, who had once hunted in Kentucky with Susannah's father, Jonathan McKay. Both young women had been homesick at first, but Susannah also had to cope with learning to live in almost total isolation and doing unaccustomed hard labor. On several occasions Nate and James helped one another with their work, and Hannah and Susannah also visited and shared their chores. Usually, however, Susannah's days had been filled with wearying work. It was only when she realized that her husband was happier than he had ever been that Susannah had accepted Kentucky as her permanent home.

Nate McIntyre turned from the ox cart on which he had loaded the last of the Campbell's few possessions that hadn't been taken from the cabin before he and a party of neighbors, alerted by Susannah, had chased away the plundering Indians. "Are ye ready to go? I'm done here," he said.

"So am I," Susannah said with a trace of sadness.

Nate untied the reins of two saddled horses and led them toward them.

"Susannah can ride Shadow," Hannah said, indicating the horse that Nate had given her as an engagement gift.

"'Twould be easier for her than trying to keep my horse in

check," Nate agreed. Hannah's tall husband, who had let his woodsman's beard grow again now that he was back in Kentucky, made a stirrup with his hands and boosted Susannah into the saddle.

Nate turned to Hannah, whose figure plainly revealed that she was due to give birth to their first child at year's end. "Ye can ride behind me." He helped his wife into place and then spoke reassuringly to Susannah. "We'll not ride fast."

Susannah laid a hand on her stomach, where only a slight thickening betrayed her own condition. The child had just begun to move, a strange fluttering sensation unlike anything that Susannah had ever experienced. Already she felt that she would give her own life for the sake of this child; she would never do anything that could harm her baby.

Seeing Nate's anxious expression, Susannah gathered the reins and almost smiled. "Oh? I suppose that means I can't race you and Hannah to the trace."

Nate looked surprised, then he grinned. Hannah smiled in relief. In the grim weeks since Susannah had found her scalped and mutilated husband, it was the first time they had heard her speak at all lightly.

She'll be all right, thank God, Hannah thought. Susannah had suffered a tragic blow, but she had her baby to consider. With God's help and in His time, Susannah would recover.

❧

Even before he and Hannah married, Nate had built and furnished his double cabin in anticipation of having a family to fill it. Its four rooms had more than enough room to accommodate Susannah and her meager goods.

"Ye can see we've fit all your goods in with no trouble, lass," Nate assured Susannah that evening. His speech had more of a rolling burr than her father's, since Nate had left his native Scotland at a much later age than had Jonathan McKay. Her father's old long-hunting companion's voice reminded

KAY CORNELIUS lives in Huntsville, Alabama. Mrs. Cornelius' talent for research and detail brings her stories to life. Her "Frontiers of Faith" historical series has been one of **Heartsong Presents** most popular series.

Books by Kay Cornelius

After days of wondering, Susannah knew the moment had come that would reveal whether she would live or die.

When the feasting was finished, Black Oak walked to the center of the lodge, stood in front of the fire, and raised his arms aloft as a signal that he was about to say something. As many as could seated themselves on the earthen floor, and the others stood around the lodge walls. All was silent as he began to speak.

Susannah's knowledge of Delaware didn't allow her to follow everything that Black Oak said. He began with an oration praising the bravery of the warriors who had raided their enemies—that much she understood, although she couldn't make out what he said about the location or identity of those enemies. By name he praised a half-dozen warriors, ending with his sons. After they had stood in turn and bowed to acknowledge Black Oak's praise, the chief motioned for Gray Wolf to come forward.

"Bring the woman here," Black Oak directed, and immediately Gray Wolf turned to Susannah, who quickly stood without aid, ignoring the hand he had extended to help her rise.

Her action sent a murmur through the villagers, and once more Susannah realized she must have unwittingly violated some tribal tradition.

Susannah and Gray Wolf stood facing Black Oak, who held a very long, very sharp knife in his raised hand. Its blade shone in the firelight as he began to chant, softly at first, and then more loudly.

For the first time that night, fear for her life gripped Susannah, and instinctively she touched her neck, groping for but not finding the comfort of her cross. *Lord, can it be Your will for my life to end here, after all?*

Susannah of her father and made her long to see him and her family again. "Hannah and me hope ye'll think of this place as home now."

They sat around the hearth, where apples roasted in the ashes of a cheery fire and Nate oversaw the joint of meat roasting on the spit.

"I do thank you both for all you've done for me, but 'tis time I made some plans for the future."

"There's no hurry," said Hannah. "'Twould be a mistake to rush into doing anything hasty. You're safe here with us."

"Am I?" Susannah raised her dark eyes and regarded Hannah steadily. "Is anyone in Kentucky really safe? James certainly wasn't—"

"James knew the risk, and he was willin' to take it," Nate interrupted. "His death won't go unavenged, I can promise ye that. There's a call out for volunteers to gather at Colonel Clark's to go into Indian Territory and wipe out the raiders' villages."

Hannah shot a startled glance at her husband. "This is the first I've heard of it. Surely you don't aim to go with them?"

Nate busied himself with turning the meat before he resumed his seat beside his wife. He avoided looking directly at her as he spoke. "How could I do otherwise? We have a score to settle with the Indians, and the sooner 'tis done, the safer Kentucky will be for us all."

Hannah's hair gleamed scarlet in the firelight, and her cheeks took on a similar hue as she turned to face her husband. "Nate McIntyre, how can you tell Susannah that she'll be safe here and then run off and leave us both to heaven knows what? 'Tis no time to be deserting us in our condition."

Nate put a placating arm around his wife's shoulders and smiled the slow, sweet smile that had so endeared him to her. "Don't ye worry, wife. It's already settled. I'll take ye and Susannah to the strongest place in these parts before I leave, and I'll not be gone long."

"But why you, Nate? Surely there must be plenty of unattached men to fight the Indians."

"The more we have, the sooner the matter will be concluded. Besides, I'll be needed to scout, since I know the Indian Territory."

"What tribes will you go against?" Susannah asked. In the shadows cast by the firelight, the high cheekbones and straight nose she had inherited from her Delaware mother looked even more prominent, and Hannah knew what her cousin must be thinking.

"The bunch that raided Bryant's Station was from several tribes—Wyandot, Shawnee, Ottawa, Chippewa..." Nate's voice trailed off and once more he stood to turn the joint of meat over the fire.

"And Delaware?"

Nate nodded. "Delaware, especially, because of those Delaware Christians that some no-good British officer ordered killed. That attack and siege at Bryant's Station back in August was a direct result of his folly."

"Many men died needlessly then," Susannah said. "You and James were fortunate to get there after the ambuscade. I keep thinking of how poor Rebecca Boone must have felt when Dan'l came home and told her that another of their sons had been killed by Indians."

Nate touched Susannah's hand and spoke quietly. "Och, ye mustn't dwell on the bad things, lass. 'Tis not good for the babe nor its mother, neither. Ye owe it to James to take care of yourself, and we'll help ye all we can to do that."

"I know you mean well," Susannah said. She had cried very little; it was as if the awful shock of coming upon her dead husband had drained her of all emotion. But now Nate's compassion brought the sting of sudden tears to her eyes.

"I suppose Nate's right," Hannah said grudgingly. "We'll be

together while he's gone, and like Uncle Adam always says, God will take care of us."

Will He? Susannah wiped her eyes with the back of her hand and fingered the wooden cross she wore on a rawhide lace around her neck. Her father had carved it for her mother before they were married. It was the only thing of her mother's she had, and it was her most precious possession. But now it gave her no comfort. The part of her being that had once so trustingly prayed seemed hollow and empty. Ever since her husband's death, Susannah had found God to seem as remote as the possibility that she would ever be truly happy again.

❧

They reached Lexington so late in the evening of a rainy November day that Susannah had only the briefest glimpse of the bustling settlement before Nate took her and Hannah to the house where, he assured them, they would stay in safety.

Mary Chandler, a plump, middle-aged widow who had turned her two-story double cabin into a boarding house to support herself, had known Nate for years and welcomed him warmly.

"This is my wife, Hannah," Nate said when Mary Chandler released him from a bear hug.

"Take off that cloak an' let me have a look at you," the woman directed.

Hannah pulled back her hood, revealing a torrent of red hair. Mary Chandler chuckled as Nate took the sodden garment from around his wife's shoulders and hung it on a peg by the door. "I see what you meant when you tole me this one was worth waitin' for her to grow up to wed," she said heartily.

Hannah looked questioningly at Nate, who grinned back at her. She looked back to Mary. "It looks like everyone in Kentucky knew that Nate intended to marry me before I did," she said with some asperity.

"Well, I reckon he didn't want to scare off a pretty young thing like you," Mary Chandler said. She then turned her attention to Susannah, who had watched the exchange in silence. "Now, who's this? Come closer so's I can see you."

"This is Susannah Campbell, Hannah's recently widowed cousin. The two of them need a safe place to stay whilst I'm with General Clark."

As Nate spoke, Susannah stepped forward into the circle of light from the fireplace, the only illumination in the room. Mary Chandler leaned forward and looked closely at her, then turned to Nate with a puzzled look. "Is she Injun?" she asked, as if Susannah couldn't answer for herself.

"Ye recall my old partner Jonathan McKay—Susannah is his daughter," Nate replied.

"I see," said Mary. She folded her arms at her waist and regarded Susannah soberly. "My Simon, may God rest his soul, set a great store by Jonny McKay. Some folks thought he'd made a big mistake when he wed your ma, but Simon allus said it was none of our concern."

Susannah felt her cheeks warm at Mary Chandler's implied criticism, but before she could think of anything to say, the woman smiled and stepped forward to take her hand. "You're welcome in this house, anyway. Is your pa fit? Nate tole me he'd not be back this way a-huntin' any more."

"He was in April when we left to come to Kentucky."

"And your ma?" Mary asked, still holding Susannah's hand in a firm grip.

"She died many years ago," Susannah replied.

Mary dropped Susannah's hand and nodded. "Aye, of course—now I recall hearin' that Jonny'd got himself a Frenchy wife—and that a good long time ago. But what am I thinkin' of, babblin' on like this when I ort to be showin' you where you stay? You're in luck that I've any spare room—and it's only because the Yarrow boys left two days ago to join up with General Clark. Of course, they'll be wantin' the room back when they return," she added.

"The ladies'll have no further need of it by then," Nate replied. "As soon as our job with the general is over, I'll be back for them."

Mary Chandler sighed heavily. "I wish you Godspeed in your task. If wipin' out their villages is the only way to keep them Injuns from botherin' us all the time, then I say get the job done, and the sooner the better."

Having delivered herself of that opinion, Mary Chandler drew a stubby candle-end from the pocket of her commodious apron and bent to light it from the fire. "'Tis growin' late, and the lot of you look like you could do with a good rest. I'll take you to the room now."

❧

By daylight, Susannah saw that Lexington was far more than the crude frontier settlement she had expected. All around the village some of the earlier log cabins were being replaced by frame and brick houses. Announced by crudely lettered signs, businesses of all types had been set up by merchants. Most of the business owners lived upstairs over their shops as she and James had done in Salisbury.

How long ago that all seems now, Susannah thought forlornly as she and Hannah completed their tour of the town and started back to Mary Chandler's. Nate had left at first light, and while his wife tried not to show her concern, Susannah knew that Hannah would worry about Nate every minute they were apart, as she also did.

One widow in the family is enough, Susannah thought. Without Nate, what would she and Hannah do?

Occupied with their separate thoughts, neither Hannah nor Susannah heard the first voices that called out as they passed a tavern, but when the words were repeated more loudly, Susannah stopped and turned to see who was saying them.

"Say, look at that Injun squaw!" a stout, red-faced man called from the doorway.

Behind him, a taller man clad in buckskins jeered derisively. "Where did ye come by that dress, squaw? Whose wife did your man scalp to git it?"

Susannah's first reaction was surprise, then shocked anger. Her mouth opened, but she found herself rendered speechless by the men's senseless attack. Before she could recover enough to speak, Hannah put herself between Susannah and the men. She shook an accusing finger at them as she spoke.

"This young woman is no squaw, but my near kin, just widowed by Indian treachery. If you're so worried about Indians, why don't you go join up with General Clark and do something to stop them?"

Susannah tugged at Hannah's arm and tried to lead her away. "It's all right," she said shakily. "The men are drunk—they don't know what they're saying."

"Drunk, are we?" roared the stout man. He took a staggering step toward them, then stopped as his companion held him back. "I can smell an Injun anytime, drunk or sober, and call her what ye will, that un's an Injun what should go back to where she came from."

"Enough, Sam," the taller man said. He looked embarrassed as he gestured to Hannah and Susannah. "You ladies had best get along home now."

"I need no second invitation to do that," Hannah murmured. Taking Susannah by the hand, they walked away rapidly, followed by the laughter of several bystanders who had gathered to watch the exchange.

Susannah was trembling all over when they reached Mary Chandler's house, and Hannah immediately made her sit down while she fetched a dipper of water. "Splash some of this on your face, too," she directed. "Mercy, don't let those drunken idiots bother you. They're not worth it."

Susannah took a few sips of water and shook her head. "Maybe not, but you seemed to be pretty bothered yourself."

Hannah compressed her lips and looked grim. "It's men like

that make me glad I don't live in town—there's too many who have little to do but drink and get into trouble."

Susannah remained silent for a moment, then she touched her hair, which she had been braiding Indian-style for the sake of convenience. "Maybe I should unbraid my hair and wear a bonnet," she said.

"No!" Hannah exclaimed with a force that startled Susannah. "Your Indian features are lovely, and to try to hide them because of what a few drunken louts said would only be giving in to them."

"I don't want to cause any trouble," Susannah said. "I'll just stay inside while we're here—I think it's safer."

When she heard of the incident, Mary Chandler reluctantly agreed with Susannah's evaluation. "It's not just the men, but some o' the women hate the sight of anyone with Injun blood, too. That's the very reason you'll not find many half-breeds livin' here in Lexington."

Susannah and Hannah both winced at the term "half-breed," which carried with it the idea that such a person was somehow inferior. It had sometimes been used to deride members of Susannah's family in Carolina, but knowing they'd have Jonathan McKay to deal with, no one had ever dared to say it to their faces.

"In any case, we'll not be here long," Hannah reassured. "Nate said the raids against the Indian towns will be carried out swiftly."

"I hope so," Susannah said, but she knew that Nate's return wouldn't completely solve her own problems. Whatever future Susannah might have, she was daily more convinced that it didn't lie in Kentucky.

❧

A few days later, on November 3, 1782, Nate McIntyre joined over a thousand other mounted men from all over Kentucky County at the place where the Licking River empties into the Ohio. Two years earlier General George Rogers Clark had led a similar raid against the Shawnees, but then Nate had been long-hunting in the western regions and had known nothing about it.

Now he looked around in awe at the show of force that had been gathered. Perhaps half of the participants were, like him, seeking to avenge the death and destruction that various Indians, particularly Shawnees, had recently caused. But from what Nate had heard others say, some hoped to gain plunder and, eventually, take the lands on which the Indians still lived under treaty.

Nate had reported to General Clark, who directed him to the formidable Simon Kenton, one of the earliest white settlers and already an almost legendary frontiersman. "Kenton's in charge of the scouts and spies. He's asked for your services."

"It's good to see you again, McIntyre," the burly Kenton greeted him. "I need you to scout for General Logan."

"Where is Logan to go?" asked Nate, who knew that General Clark's strategy called for the force to be divided.

"To the Shawnee towns on the Great Miami River, the Piqua towns—and Peter Loramie's trading post."

Nate raised his eyebrows. "Is Loramie still supplying the Indians? I thought he had been persuaded to reform."

Kenton laughed without humor. "Not while there's still profit to be made in selling liquor and arms, I fear. I've seen too many of that man's bullets used against my friends—I know what he's up to, and he'll keep on doing it until we destroy his supplies."

"All right. I'll go find General Logan now—and see you when this is over."

Kenton nodded. "Be careful out there, McIntyre. We can't afford to lose any more men like you."

❧

Gray Wolf stood, statue-still, and watched the two white men, each sitting tall in the saddle, who were obviously scouting the territory. Beneath yellow and vermilion stripes of war paint, the young man's expression showed his concern. Quietly he prepared his rifle, raised it to his shoulder, and moved it toward his target. But then, still out of his rifle's range, the men suddenly wheeled and rode away at a gallop.

Disappointed, Gray Wolf lowered his rifle. He wanted to pursue them, but his better judgment told him it would be folly to do so. The riders would already be far away by the time he could ford the Little Miami River, and the vain pursuit would only rob him of valuable time.

Gray Wolf climbed down from the rock and considered the meaning of what he had seen. His arms were stiff from the cold and he moved them rapidly across his chest, then stomped his moccasined feet until he felt the blood warming them again.

The rumors must be true, after all, he thought with a heavy heart. It was said that hundreds of *schwannack** stood ready to cross the Ohio and make directly for the land between the Greater Miami and Little Miami Rivers, where Black Oak had decided to wait out the winter in the hope that spring would bring better times. Now, however, it was obvious that the whole village must move quickly if they hoped to avoid a fight against overwhelming odds.

Gray Wolf untied his dark bay horse, formerly the property of a British soldier who had once ventured too close, and swung into the saddle. He'd grown up riding bareback, but once he'd sat in a regular saddle, Gray Wolf never wanted to ride any other way. He secured his rifle in its sling above the horse's withers and, with heels and reins, urged the animal to a flat run. Every minute counted now, and the sooner he reached the village with his warning, the better would be their chance of survival.

≈

Nate McIntyre had seen the solitary figure first and pointed him out to his scouting companion, John Mason. "Shawnee,

---

*Delaware term for bad white people.

ye think?" he asked.

John, who had barely escaped with his scalp when captured by the Shawnee a few years back, shook his head. "Not likely. In fact…" He squinted in an attempt to see better, then sighed. "I ain't even sure that's an Injun at all—he's too tall, and his hair's mighty light-colored."

"Many Delaware are tall. He could have lightened his hair, and that's certainly Indian wampum around his neck," Nate said.

"Look out—he's raising his rifle!" John Mason warned.

"We're out of his range, but we might as well go, anyway— we've seen enough here," Nate said, and immediately the men turned their horses.

His scouting partner also knew the futility of further exposing themselves to danger, so he didn't question Nate's actions. It would be a waste of their time to follow the man they'd seen. He might not be alone, and they were too wary to be led into an ambush. Though he would no doubt warn his own village, there were still dozens of others that would, in the coming days, feel the sting of the white man's revenge.

ze

Black Oak heard his adopted son's report in stony-faced silence. He made no comment even after Gray Wolf finished speaking and stood before him, silently awaiting the chief's orders.

"Call the people together," Black Oak said at length. "Tell them to prepare for a long journey."

"Where will we go, Father?"

"To the village of my brother Running Beaver in the east."

There we will exchange one danger for another, Gray Wolf thought, but he said nothing. One never disputed the chief's word or gave any opinion of it unless asked, and that was seldom the case. Gray Wolf brought his fist to his heart in the traditional sign of obedience and turned to leave.

"Wait!"

Gray Wolf stopped at the door of the chief's lodge. "Yes, Father?"

"Tell the women to dig pits in the woods and bury what they cannot carry. One day we return to this place."

Gray Wolf nodded. "It will be done."

But as he left his father's presence, Gray Wolf feared in his heart that it would not be so; his people had probably seen the last of their pleasant village by the Little Miami.

❧

Susannah had been in Lexington a week when she began to feel the first vague ache radiate through her belly. As the day wore on and Susannah's aches became more unpleasant, Hannah noticed that something was amiss and quickly guessed the probable cause.

"You must go to bed and stay there. Lie quietly and rest," Hannah told her, although Susannah had done less work in the past two weeks than she'd done since she'd come to Kentucky. Certainly here in Mary Chandler's house there was no land to be cleared or cane to be cut and no bawling cow to be milked. She had helped Mary card and spin some wool, but that was hardly work at all, compared to the hard labor she had been doing.

"Why am I having these pains?" Susannah asked Hannah, who had learned many healing arts from her mother.

"Show me exactly where it hurts."

"Here." Susannah pressed her barely swollen womb, then moaned as a cramp seized her.

"It may be nothing," Hannah said, but her frown betrayed her concern. "I wish I had my physick with me, but mayhap I can find a healer in the village that can give me something to help you."

"Please hurry," Susannah said as another pain ripped through her belly.

Calling for Mary Chandler to sit with Susannah, Hannah hastily donned her cloak and went out into the frosty morning air. All the way to and from the house of the healer Mary had told her about, her lips moved in silent prayer for Susannah and her baby.

Dear God, let me help her keep her baby, Hannah prayed. But the moment she returned to the house and heard her cousin's wrenching, keening cries, she feared that she was too late, and that the worst must have happened.

Mary Chandler looked up when Hannah came into the room and shook her head. "She's bleedin' right bad," she whispered.

Hannah produced the vial she had brought from the healer. "This will help," she said. "We'll need some linen strips to bind her tight."

"Oh, Hannah, I lost my baby," Susannah said raggedly. "First James, and now this. Let me die, too—I've nothing to live for, nothing—"

"Hush!" Hannah spoke sharply and raised Susannah's head with one hand. "God is the final judge of that, but as long as I have any say in the matter, you'll be with us a good long while yet. Drink this and be still."

Susannah gagged a bit, but she managed to swallow most of the bitter liquid. She closed her eyes and lay back, clutching Hannah's hand as if it were her lifeline. By the time Mary Chandler returned with the linen bandages, Susannah had fallen into an exhausted sleep.

Mary knelt beside her and raised questioning eyes to Hannah. "Will she be all right?"

Hannah inclined her head. "I think so. My cousin is a strong young woman."

"What do you suppose took her babe like that?" Mary asked.

Hannah shrugged. "I don't know. Sometimes these things just happen. My mother always said we mustn't question God's wisdom."

Mary looked at Susannah's face, sad even in repose. "Aye,

but to lose a husband and then a child in so short a time—'tis a heavy burden to bear. In her place, I'd question God, too."

"Susannah has strong faith," Hannah said.

"I hope you're right—she has plenty need of it," murmured Mary Chandler.

two

Just over two weeks after the expedition against the Indians had crossed the Ohio River, its work was finished. For the second time George Rogers Clark had led a force against the Indian towns of Chillicothe and Piqua Town. Every Shawnee *wegiwa* had been burned, starting grass fires that destroyed everything for miles around. All food had either been loaded on horses to be returned to Kentucky or burned in the *wegiwa* fires.

Benjamin Logan's force had burned Upper and Lower Piqua Town on the Great Miami and utterly destroyed Peter Loramie's store. They had met little resistance, and only one man of the more than a thousand who had set out had been wounded, shot in the arm by a lone Indian from Piqua Town on the Mad River.

Yet when the party returned to the rallying point at the mouth of the Licking River, Nate McIntyre wasn't the only man who felt their victory had been less than complete.

"There ort to a'been Injuns in all them places," John Mason said.

"I heared they knowed we was a-comin' and decided it was time to jine their brothers on the other side of the big river," said Tim Harless, who had scouted with Simon Kenton for General Clark.

"They knew we were coming, all right," Nate McIntyre said, "but I doubt they went very far, and probably not west but east. They wouldn't leave behind some of the things we found if they'd a-gone on a long travel."

"Well, at least they can't live offen that land for many a

moon," John Mason declared. "We gave 'em somethin' to think about, anyhow."

"That's right—and I don't know about you boys, but I'm pretty nigh ready to go home," Tim Harless said.

"We all are," Nate McIntyre agreed, and half an hour later, when the force had been officially dismissed, he was among the first to head back toward Lexington.

❧

Gray Wolf always sought out the highest point of land to survey any place that his people stopped, even for one night, for possible danger. Only after Gray Wolf approved a site would Black Oak give the order to make camp. For three days and nights they had stayed on the move, finally reaching the land where Black Oak expected to be received by his brother, Running Beaver. But the village was deserted, and the appearance of their lodges suggested that the inhabitants had fled in haste from some danger.

They had then pressed on to the south, where the land was more gently rolling than hilly and less densely forested than they would prefer. But the area had two great advantages: it was dotted with limestone caves, and it was near the Ohio River.

Gray Wolf shaded his eyes with the back of his hand and squinted to the south, where a heavy stand of trees by the shore prevented him from seeing the river itself. But it was there, and from it the people could sustain themselves through the long winter ahead.

He turned back and went to the waiting chief. "This is a good place," he said.

Black Oak nodded. "We will stop here, then," he said. "Send the women and children to gather wood and make a safe place for the horses."

Gray Wolf put his fist to his heart, but did not leave. "The people are hungry, Father. For two days they have not eaten."

"We must save the little grain we have left. The warriors will go out after game. Tonight we eat meat in this new place."

Gray Wolf hesitated a moment before asking the question that had been on his mind for some time. "Will we raid on the river?"

Black Oak barely nodded. "We must live," he said. "Now go. The shadows lengthen—the time to gather wood grows short."

Nate McIntyre neared Lexington on the last day of November, his spirits undampened by the heavy downpour through which he rode. All the way back from the rendezvous point, he'd been considering how he and Hannah could best help her cousin Susannah. Her most immediate need, a safe place to stay, could easily be arranged by adding a room to their cabin for her and the baby. If Susannah should remarry, they could always use the room for their own children.

No, Nate thought, *when* she remarries would be more likely, given the shortage of women on the frontier and the number of bachelors in need of a helpmeet. For many years he had been counted in that number, but God had led Hannah Stone, nearly half his age, to agree to marry him, and soon he would be a real family man himself.

Nate smiled, thinking of the child that would bless their marriage. They would welcome a babe of either sex. A first-born son would carry on the McIntyre name, while a daughter would be a help and comfort to her mother. And in any case, it didn't matter, since they hoped to have other children—

Poor James Campbell, Nate thought. He would never see his child, who would come into the world half-orphaned. Still, having to think of her babe's welfare would help Susannah through the coming months.

Nate shook himself, and rain sluiced from his hat. He'd be thoroughly chilled by the time he finally reached Mary

Chandler's house and warm fire. The thought that Hannah waited for him both warmed and spurred him on.

❧

As soon as the first of the fighting men began to arrive back in Lexington to noisy welcomes, Susannah excused herself and went upstairs saying she was tired and needed to rest, but Hannah realized her cousin hadn't wanted to intrude on Nate's return.

"You're lettin' all the heat out and the rain in," Mary Chandler grumbled good-naturedly as Hannah kept going to and opening the hinged window, watching out for Nate.

"He'll be cold and wet when he gets here—I'll build up the fire." Hannah stooped to pick up a slab of wood, but Mary stopped her and bent to the task herself.

"You don't need to be liftin' anything heavy in your condition," warned Mary. "I'm goin' off to the kitchen now. Likely Nate and the Yarrow boys'll be needin' a hot meal when they come back."

A few minutes later, Nate knocked at the door, and the moment she opened the door to him, Hannah threw herself into Nate's arms.

"Ye'll get all wet," Nate began to protest, but her arms around his neck and her lips on his soon stopped him.

"Mayhap I should go away more often," Nate said when Hannah finally let him go.

"No!" Hannah exclaimed. "I never intend to spend another day out of your sight as long as we live."

Nate took his wife's hands in his and looked down into her tear-bright eyes.

"What's happened?" he asked, aware that her agitation had to be due to more than pleasure at his return.

"Oh, Nate…," she began, then stopped as if she lacked the will to say what had to be told.

Nate felt a thrill of alarm and grasped Hannah's forearms.

"Are you all right? Nothing is amiss with the baby?"

"Not ours, thank God," she said quickly. Relieved, Nate hugged her, then pulled back to look in her face.

"It must be Susannah, then?"

Hannah nodded. "She miscarried about a week after you left. There was no reason for it that any of us could see and naught could be done to stop it."

Nate furrowed his brow and pulled at his beard. "How is she? Will she recover?"

"She was quite weak for a few days, but she's much better now. However, I'm some worried about her frame of mind."

"I don't wonder that the poor girl wouldna find much to be happy about these days. In time, mayhap—"

Hannah stopped Nate by laying her hand lightly on his lips, then stood tiptoe to kiss him again. "That's enough talk of sad things. You must get out of those wet buckskins before you take a chill, and likely you're hungry. Mary has hot food ready for you."

Nate smiled fondly at his wife and kissed her on the forehead. "Ah, my practical Hannah," he said. "Who would ever have thought that ye'd take such good care of me?"

"You don't fool me for a moment, Nate McIntyre—I know good and well that's the main reason you took me to wife. I'll bring in your dry clothes now—you can put them on whilst I help Mary finish up the cooking."

Nate nodded. "I thank ye. But soon's I change clothes, I'd like to see Susannah."

A few minutes later Hannah called softly from the doorway of the room where her cousin lay with her face turned to the wall. "Susannah? Nate's back. He wants to talk to you."

Susannah turned to look at Hannah, whose face shone with happiness. She felt, then quickly tried to suppress, a stab of jealousy. *Of course Hannah is happy. Her husband's come back to her—but mine never will.*

Susannah sat up on the pallet and reached for her slippers. "I told you Nate'd be all right," she said. "Is he downstairs?"

"No, I'm right here," Nate replied from Hannah's side. "No need for you to disturb yourself."

"I'm not an invalid—I'm quite able to come downstairs," Susannah said tartly.

Hannah touched her husband's hand. "I'll help Mary put out the food. The both of you can come down in a bit."

Nate nodded. "Aye—I've not had a hot meal in some days," he said as Hannah left them.

Susannah swayed slightly as she stood, and Nate reached out to steady her. "I'm all right," she said sharply. "I got up too sudden, and my head turned around—it's fine now."

Nate stared at the wide-planked pine floor as if seeking some words of consolation, then looked back at Susannah. "I'm sorry about—" he began, then stopped. "I mean, Hannah told me what happened whilst I was gone. I wish things had been different for ye."

Susannah nodded. "So do I. But as Hannah keeps reminding me, I must go on living, whether I want to or not."

"Ye've had more sorrow than a body ought to have to bear, and all coming at the same time. But ye maun know that ye'll want for naught as long as Hannah and I live. Ye have a home with us for as long as ye like."

It was one of the longest declarations Susannah had ever heard Nate deliver, but his sympathy was almost harder to bear than indifference would have been. While Nate was away, Susannah had become even more determined to make her own way in the world. She had resolved not to allow anyone else to decide for her how—or even where—she should live.

Susannah squared her shoulders and spoke purposefully. "I thank you—I appreciate all the help you and Hannah have given me. I don't know what I'd have done without you. But I don't intend to impose on you any longer."

Surprised, Nate looked closely at Susannah. The tilt of her chin and the almost defiant look in her eyes made it clear that she'd made up her mind to do something that didn't concern the McIntyres. "Have ye some plans, then?"

Susannah nodded. "I know what I want to do, but I'll need help in the doing of it."

"If I can be of service, ye know I will. What is it ye wish?"

"I want to go home. I want to go back to Carolina."

Nate pulled on his beard and shook his head. "I don't rightly know how that can be done just yet, lass. Ye canna travel alone, nor am I free to take ye."

"I don't expect you to, but traders and settlers travel back and forth all the time. Just find me a party to go with, and I'll be out of your way."

"Ye're not in our way, lass—and I doubt ye're thinking clear about this thing, neither. Instead, let me write Jonathan McKay. He'll come and fetch ye home soon as he can—"

"No!" Susannah spoke vehemently. "My father has concerns of his own to look after, and anyway, it'd be weeks before he'd get a letter, and even longer before he could get here."

"Winter's coming on," Nate pointed out. "Only trappers travel much after November, and they'll mostly make for the western lands. None will be heading south."

"What about the flatboats?" Susannah asked. "Mary Chandler was telling me that half the people who now live in Lexington came in from Virginia on the Ohio River."

"That's true, but flatboats usually travel downriver with the current, not against it. Very few people try to make the return trip."

"But some do, don't they?"

"Aye, some do. It takes four men to pole, and ye'd only get as far as the Kanawha River. That'd still leave ye a good ways off from Carolina."

"It can be done, though," Susannah said firmly.

"Aye, it *can* be done. But 'tis a long, hard trip, and sometimes Indians hae been known to raid the flatboats. Like I said, ye'd best wait for your father, lass."

Susannah's soft brown eyes implored Nate as she took a step closer and put her hand lightly on his forearm. "I must go, Nate. I can't stay here another half year. Help me sell the property, and I'll have cash money to pay my passage."

"Are ye sure ye want to sell that land, Susannah? 'Tis a prime claim, and James set a great store by it—"

"And so did I, but he's not going to have use of it, and I don't think I could stand to live there ever again. I want to go home to Carolina, Nate."

Susannah had somehow managed to hold back her tears, but now her voice broke and she averted her face as she fought for control.

Defeated by her tears, Nate sighed and shrugged. "All right, Susannah. I'll see what can be done."

❧

They stayed in Lexington one more day, while Nate made inquiries in every shop and tavern. At last he found William Hunter, a trader who was leaving by flatboat the next week for Virginia with his family to visit relatives and return with fresh stores.

"I'll welcome another female aboard," his wife declared when William seemed reluctant to allow Susannah to go with them. With four lively young boys to look after, Caroline Hunter had rarely had the leisure to cultivate feminine friendships. When she learned that their prospective passenger was a bereaved widow who had recently suffered a miscarriage, she was even more determined to have her along. Finally, her husband threw up his hands in surrender and agreed that Susannah Campbell could travel with them, provided that she brought along her own stores and paid in hard coin.

As soon as the arrangements had been made, they rode back

to Nate and Hannah's homestead. Susannah was glad that she wouldn't have much time to think about the possible consequences of what she was doing as she packed her few belongings and made ready to join the Hunters.

The next day, Nate sold the Campbell's land warrant and returned with a stack of gold coins which he warned Susannah to hide, lest she be robbed of them.

"I'll help you sew them in the waist-casing of your petticoat," said Hannah, who had learned the trick from Mary Chandler. ("Us lone women have t' take care o' ourselves, for none other will," Mary had declared when she heard what Susannah intended to do.)

"When ye get to the Greenbrier River, find lodgings and wait for your father to come for ye," Nate instructed Susannah for at least the fifth time. "Ye mustn't be travelin' on the road alone, under any account."

"I understand," Susannah said meekly. She would have agreed to almost anything to get away from Kentucky and its sad memories.

"I hope ye do," said Nate, who was still not convinced that he should let Susannah leave Kentucky alone. "I maun see to the stock now—I'll be back in directly."

"As soon as you get home, you must send us all the news of the Yadkin neighborhood," Hannah said. "I want to know how our families are faring and who's gotten married, and who's had babies—"

Hannah stopped suddenly, aware that she might have inadvertently caused Susannah pain by mentioning babies.

"Do our folks know the news about you and Nate?"

Hannah nodded. "I think Nate wrote Father as soon as we knew— but with the uncertainty of the mail 'twixt here and Carolina, you'll probably get to the Yadkin before Nate's letter."

"Uncle Joshua will be beside himself," Susannah said. "Like

as not, he'll be here come spring." As she spoke the words, Susannah realized that she should have had her baby in the spring. She turned aside, but not before Hannah saw her tears and reached out to embrace her.

"I know 'tis hard," Hannah said softly. "But you'll always have God's help. Scripture says God waits for us to call on His name."

"I scarcely know what to ask Him for myself," Susannah said, "but if you think it'll help, I'll pray for you and Nate— and for your baby."

"It always helps," Hannah assured her. "And you can be sure you'll always have our prayers, as well."

❧

Black Oak's people had settled into their new village, temporary though they all hoped it to be, and by the time of the first snowfall, they had built enough lodges to protect them from the cold. However, some were far from satisfied. The old ones sat together in the evenings and murmured of the days when the land to the south had been theirs to range on as far as they liked. Then, there had been many herds of buffalo, and licks everywhere were filled with game.

But then the white man had come and taken away the land, a piece at a time, and with the settlers had come cattle that ate the cane that formerly fed the buffalo. The white men had killed thousands of animals for no more reason than they were there, not even bothering to dress out the meat, and now the buffalo herds had fled in terror before the spreading waves of homesteaders.

Blood had been shed on both sides, yet nothing had seemed to stop the relentless white onslaught, not feathered arrows, not rifle bullets, and especially not the treaties that their chiefs had made but which few understood and even fewer honored.

While the men complained and the women gossiped, Black Oak sat in council with his warrior sons, Little Oak and

Running Fox; three other village elders; and Gray Wolf, his adopted—and some thought most favored—son.

"We have no choice but to go to the river again, Father," said Little Oak, whose short stature never prevented him from making bold proposals. "Our people must have stores, and soon the snow flies and the cold wind from the north brings sickness on its wings."

Running Fox nodded in agreement. "We need more rifles and more bullets and powder."

The oldest of the council members turned on him with scorn. "In the old days the Lenni-Lenape brought down the buffalo with a single arrow. What is this talk of guns and bullets? They are white men's weapons, not ours."

"So once it was, Two Streams," Black Oak said, "but even you know that has not been the way of it for many cycles of the seasons. Our people need the food stores in the white man's boats. If they also carry his guns and bullets and powder, then we take them as well."

"So we will go against them, Father?" Gray Wolf asked, speaking quietly what the others had talked around, but dared not to ask directly.

"Yes, my son. You will lead the raid. Choose five others to go with you and wait for a boat at the narrows. Prepare to attack at dawn. The *schwannack* will be heavy with sleep then. Make sure their guards will not have time to sound an alarm." Black Oak looked at Two Streams, then back to Gray Wolf. "Use arrows and tomahawks, in the old way."

Running Fox leaned forward, his eyes gleaming. "What about prisoners?"

"We need no other mouths to feed," Black Oak said firmly. "There will not be prisoners."

At the tone of dismissal in the chief's voice, the men stood and saluted him, touching their fists to their chests before going out into the still night air.

It's warm for December, Gray Wolf thought. *Might that be a good sign?*

Old Gashega would have known, but the *schwannack* had killed him before he had fully trained his son, Wanega. The boy strutted and pretended to have powerful medicine, but he'd never fooled Gray Wolf into thinking he knew what he was talking about. In the old days, Wanega would not have been tolerated. In the old days—

Gray Wolf shook his head. "I sound like the old women," he muttered, then made for the lodge of Dark Moon. He would make sure that all was well with her before he chose the warriors and readied them for their task.

~

Although Susannah was determined to leave Kentucky and intended to do so by any means possible, she was a bit taken aback at her first sight of the vessel that she would entrust with her life for a journey of several hundred miles on the Ohio and Kanawha Rivers.

She and the Hunters had traveled for two days before reaching the site where the flatboat sat on logs, ready to be launched into the Ohio River. A rectangle some sixty feet long and thirty feet wide with enclosed areas at either end, the unlikely vessel reminded Susannah of a slightly larger version of the ferry that Hannah's father, Joshua Stone, had long operated on the Yadkin River in North Carolina.

"We'll stay in that end, and the stores will ride in the other," explained Mrs. Hunter, who had made the trip to Virginia and back three other times.

"I didn't ask the gal if she could handle a rifle," William Hunter said, and Susannah couldn't tell whether he jested or not.

"I could if I had to," Susannah replied, but she found it hard to imagine that she would pull the trigger if it meant harming another human.

Laughter shook Mr. Hunter's ample belly. "Aye, well, with nine of us men on board, I doubt we'll have need of your services, after all." Then his smile faded and he spoke more seriously. "More likely, I should've asked if you could swim. If there's trouble, you might have to."

Susannah thought of how cold the December river waters were likely to be and shivered. "I grew up on the Yadkin River in North Carolina—I think I could swim before I could walk. But I never tried it in this kind of weather."

William Hunter nodded. "Nor should you have to. Mind you, I expect no trouble after what General Clark and General Logan did to those Shawnees a few weeks ago. But in case of an Injun attack, remember to keep your head down. Get into the water as soon as you can and make for the south shore—the Kentucky side of the river."

Susannah's sleeping pallet was put beside Caroline Hunter's in the center of the living quarters, with the male Hunters circling them in a show of security. Susannah soon realized that the two younger boys would be of little use in an emergency, and the older two preferred to sleep in the other end of the boat, where the stores were, saying someone should guard them. With two others of the men posted as guards fore and aft, only three men of fighting age and ability remained in the living quarters at night.

Susannah had no reason to question their safety in the first few days of their voyage. The weather was fair and only moderately cold, and the net harvested twice a day yielded a variety of fish which Caroline Benjamin used to supplement the hardtack, jerky, nuts, and dried fruit already on board. At sundown, they poled to the shore, where the men tied the flatboat for the night and hunted fresh game for their supper. Usually they returned with wild turkey, rabbits, and squirrel, some of which was made into stew while the rest was roasted so that it could be eaten sooner. Because the nights were cold, they slept on the boat. At first light they were on their way again.

"This seems an ideal way to travel," Susannah told Caroline Benjamin on the third day of the journey. "We came in overland through the Gap last spring. I'd never want to make that trip in the wintertime."

"We came that same way ourself—let's see, when was it? William Jr. was just walking good, and Eddie was a babe in my arms, so it must a-been—"

Her voice trailed off as she tried to make calculations on her fingers, then frowned and gave up the effort. "I never was much for numbers," she confessed, "but Mr. Hunter can tell you the year. Anyhow, 'twas not so long ago that I've forgot how hard the trip was, which is why I told my man I'd not go back to Virginny any other way but by boat."

"You've never been bothered by Indians on any of your trips?" Susannah asked.

Caroline Hunter shook her head with such emphasis that her chin quivered. "Depends on what you mean by 'bothered,'" she said. "Down toward the loops and turns in the river, we keep a sharp lookout, but the only Injuns we ever seen there stayed on their side and minded their own business."

Susannah looked out at the expanse of water to the left side of the boat, which hugged the Kentucky side on the right as they made their way northeast. "The Ohio is the widest river I ever saw," she said. "You could see Indians coming from that side a long way off—in plenty of time to make for the Kentucky shore, I'd think."

"It's wide here, all right, but they's plenty of places where the river narrows—and that's where we have to keep a sharp lookout," put in Eddie Hunter, who had overheard Susannah's remark and replied to it before his mother could.

"We'll come to such a bend tomorrow, as a matter of fact," Caroline Hunter said. "But don't let it bother you none—we'll be all right, just as we allus have been."

A sudden premonition chilled Susannah, and absently she touched the cross around her neck as if seeking some protection from it. "I hope you're right," she said.

That night Susannah lay awake on her pallet long after the others' even breathing told her that everyone else slept. The starry skies that had so enchanted her on the previous nights had been blotted out by milky clouds, and a fresh wind sent a scattering of ghostly whitecaps dancing across the water. As she had done countless times in the weeks since her husband's death and the loss of her child, Susannah shut her eyes and tried to pray. However, it made her feel no closer to God, and even the Shepherd's Prayer seemed like vain repetition.

Something is about to happen. Susannah felt it was so, but could not say what was going to occur, or even how she knew that it would. At the very core of her being Susannah felt a strange new sensation. Not fear, but a hollowness, a waiting for a nameless, faceless something that she knew would somehow change everything.

You are fancying things again, she told herself. *You mustn't be foolish.*

Susannah turned on her side and tried to match Caroline Hunter's even breathing. Although she had not thought it possible, Susannah eventually fell into a deep sleep as the flatboat drifted through the silent night toward the most dangerous part of the narrowing Ohio River.

three

Susannah awoke with a start and sat upright. In the murky pre-dawn light, Caroline Hunter still lay asleep, as did the youngest of her sons. The men were gone, however.

When the faint sound that must have wakened her was repeated, Susannah rose and looked out on the deck from the shelter doorway. To her surprise, since it was not yet daylight, the polemen at each corner of the flatboat already bent in unison, and they had already left the shore and moved into the main channel.

"Get back inside," warned Eddie Hunter in a whisper.

Susannah kept her voice equally low. "What's happening?"

"Nothin' yet," Eddie replied. "If we're lucky, nothin' will. Next few minutes'll tell that tale."

"Shouldn't the others be awakened?" Susannah asked.

"Let Ma sleep long's she can—and the brats'd just make noise and be in the way. Keep 'em all quiet long as you can."

"All right," Susannah agreed. She returned to the pallet and lay down, straining to hear the slightest evidence of trouble, but all was quiet. After a while she sat up and pulled on the heavy shoes that she'd worn on the overland trip from North Carolina and in which she'd worked alongside James. Then she added her cloak to the long-sleeved dress, over two petticoats, in which she had slept. Although the weather the past few days had been unusually moderate for December, the morning air had a sharp edge, and Susannah wondered if she should add wood to the fire which, as usual, had been banked for the night.

She had already reached the doorway on her way to ask

William Hunter about it when he unaccountably doubled up and slumped to the deck. At almost the same instant, the man poling on the front of the left side of the flatboat let out a startled exclamation just as he, too, fell. Before Susannah had time to react, she heard a splash and turned just as the rear poleman fell into the water. This time, she saw the arrow that had pierced his neck and knew with chilling certainty that the flatboat was under Indian attack.

Immediately Susannah turned and ran back into the shelter. "Wake up!" she cried. "Indians!"

Caroline Hunter sprang to her feet with an agility that surprised Susannah. "Boys, see to the rifles," she ordered quietly. Without a word her younger sons threw off their covers and ran to the corner, where rifles stood in a stack, alongside already-filled powder horns.

"What should we do?" Susannah asked Caroline.

"You might try prayin'," the woman said calmly. "But you'd better grab one of them axes, too, in case the savages get this far."

At that moment the flatboat rocked, and Susannah realized it must have been rammed. The vessel was far too sturdy to be turned over by such a maneuver, but it indicated that those who had shot arrows at the polemen were now close enough to board the flatboat.

As in a dream Susannah watched Caroline Hunter and her sons ram charges down the barrel of their Kentucky rifles and knew her trembling hands could never load a rifle, much less fire it. Instead, she took up one of the axes that the boys used to cut firewood and edged toward the doorway.

"Get away from there!" Caroline Hunter cried out, and Susannah quickly retreated.

On the deck, the noise of rifle fire shattered the calm of the morning, followed by a confusion of yells and screams and the sound of a scuffle to the front of the flatboat. Instinctively

Caroline Hunter and Susannah huddled together beside the stacked arms.

"The Injuns'll kill us all!" the youngest Hunter boy whimpered.

"Hush!" his mother said, just as Eddie Hunter entered the shelter. His expression was grim and his face ashen in the growing light. "We gotta leave, now!"

"But how?" Susannah asked.

"Through the fishin' hold, here—and hurry!" Eddie lifted aside the heavy logs covering a rectangular hole in the flatboat floor from which fishing nets hung. He slashed through the netting, releasing the half-dozen fish trapped there, and turned to Susannah. "You first," he said. "Take off that cloak—it'll just weigh you down."

Susannah looked at the dank river water beneath her and noted the narrowness of the opening. "It's not wide enough," she protested, but Eddie Hunter pushed her toward it.

"Yes, it is. Now, go!"

Aware that she had no other choice, Susannah hesitated only a moment before she sat on the floor, dangled her legs into the water, and then took a deep breath and slid, feet first, into the Ohio River.

Susannah expected the water to be cold, but she wasn't prepared for the shock of its icy grip, nor had she realized how dark it would be underneath the boat. She treaded water for a moment, trying to get her bearings, then something hit her shoulder, and she realized that Caroline or one of the younger Hunter boys must have followed her. Even without the cloak, Susannah's wet skirts pulled her down, and too late she realized that she should also have removed her heavy shoes. With difficulty she leaned forward far enough to move her arms in a clumsy dog-paddle.

Amplified through the water, terrible sounds told her of the scene that must be taking place on the flatboat deck.

I must get away from underneath the boat, Susannah realized. She pulled herself through the water just beneath the surface, aiming for the light, where she could rise long enough to take a breath. Long before she reached it, Susannah's chest burned and she felt her lungs must surely burst. In her youth Susannah's brothers and sisters had held contests to see who could hold their breath the longest underwater, and Susannah had never won any of them.

They should see me now, she thought grimly. Surely she had gone whole minutes longer than she'd ever been without taking in precious air—and as she felt numbness creep in her legs and a deep blackness threatening her consciousness, Susannah knew she must surface immediately or die.

I want to live, she acknowledged. Even though a dozen Indians might be waiting to kill her, she would take the chance. She had to breathe.

The instant her head broke the surface of the water, Susannah gulped a mouthful of precious air. She opened her eyes and tried to gauge her position, but her vision was too blurred to make out any details. She could see and hear enough to know that the Indians were still on the flatboat. Susannah turned her body in the water and looked for Caroline Hunter and her boys, but they were nowhere in sight.

If anything happens, make for the Kentucky shore, William Hunter had told Susannah, but in the confusion of her escape and near-drowning, Susannah had no idea in which direction Kentucky lay. Over her shoulder she saw only open water. There was no Indian canoe on the side of the flatboat that she could see, leading her to believe that she had somehow gotten turned around in the water. Since the Indians must have landed their canoe on the side of the boat parallel to the Indian Territory, the fact that she no longer saw it convinced Susannah that the line of trees she could see a few hundred yards away must mark the Kentucky shore.

"Lord, give me the strength to get there," Susannah said aloud. Filling her lungs with life-giving air, she ducked below the surface once more and with all her might she pulled her body through the water. Twice more Susannah surfaced to breathe, and each time she wondered if she would ever reach the elusive shore. When on the second breath the trees seemed no closer, Susannah realized with a stab of terror that the river current had turned her so that she was swimming parallel to the shore, not toward it.

I can't fight this current, Susannah thought wearily, but from somewhere a voice told her otherwise.

I am with you. You can do this.

Susannah thought of her Uncle Adam Craighead, a minister who preached that the God who numbers even the hairs of our heads would let none die before it was time. When both James and her baby had been taken from her, Susannah had thought that she wanted to die, too. But now, even when the numbing cold threatened to steal away her consciousness, she fought to live.

With all my strength, I will try.

Laboriously Susannah turned herself until the tug of the current on her side told her that her strokes would now take her toward the shore. With arms that had all but ceased to feel the cold and legs that barely moved, Susannah swam on.

❧

Gray Wolf put the last of the plunder from the flatboat in his canoe and nodded to Running Fox, who stood beside him on the deck. "We have taken all we can—there is just room in Little Oak's canoe for you. Light a brand and fire the boat as you leave."

Running Fox frowned. "Here is much good wood. We could come back later and break it up, make many fires for winter."

Gray Wolf shook his head. "No! If *schwannack* get here first, they bring others and use boat again. We burn it."

"They not get away." Running Fox made a gesture that took in the grisly scene of slaughter, carried out without a single casualty to the raiders.

"Burn it," Gray Fox repeated. "I stay and watch."

Running Fox opened his mouth as if he would protest, then silently turned away and went into the shelter, where he emerged moments later holding a piece of firewood he had kindled to flame from the ashes of the fire. The plunder they hadn't been able to carry had been left in a jumble on the deck beside the wall of the living quarters. Running Fox thrust the wood into the center of the pile and fanned it until tongues of flame ignited. Soon the stack of goods flamed high, first scorching and then setting fire to the living quarters wall, then to the flatboat's flooring.

"Go now." Gray Wolf watched Running Fox clamber into the other canoe and push away from the smoking flatboat before he eased his oars into the river current and began to pull hard for the shore from which they had come. No one lived on this part of the river, but smoke from the burning boat would alert any *schwannack* who might happen to be anywhere near, and some might be foolish enough to pursue the raiding party into the Indian Territory.

Near the shore, Gray Wolf stopped and looked back to the flatboat. He knew how many bodies lay on the flatboat deck, and from counting the pallets inside the shelter, he also knew that at least four people must have left the flatboat through the fish-hold cover. Given the cold temperature of the river, Gray Wolf presumed that very likely that they must have drowned almost as soon as they hit the water. However, only one body, that of a woman, had surfaced.

Thinking of the woman's strangely peaceful countenance, Gray Wolf frowned and bent again to the oars. Once he had known a woman with yellow hair like that, a woman who had worn a blue dress and who had held him to her heart. Now, however, that woman had become only a faint memory, like all his life before he had become Black Oak's son. *Trying to think past this present time is not good,* Dark Moon had once told him, and Gray Wolf seldom did.

He looked downstream, where Running Fox and Little Oak were already unloading their canoe. The other two were still making for the shore, as was Gray Wolf, although he was some distance west of them. With one last pull of the oars he touched the rocky bottom. He maneuvered the canoe close enough to shore so he could leap the remaining distance, then turned and hauled it up on the shore without getting his feet wet. Laden as it was with plunder, the canoe was too heavy to pull very far; he would have to start unloading it before he could drag it completely out of the water.

Preoccupied with his task, Gray Wolf almost stumbled over a still form that lay barely on the shore, face down, arms outstretched as if still reaching for land.

Another drowned schwannack woman from the flatboat, he thought. But this one was smaller than the body of the woman he'd just seen, and her hair, rather than being light, was as dark and rich as Fair Star's.

Gray Wolf knelt and turned her over, using his arms rather than his foot, as he might have done with a man. He drew back in surprise. This woman was much younger than the other, and with her darker skin and high cheekbones, she looked almost entirely Indian. Unlike the other woman, however, this one's face showed no sign of peace, but rather the ravages of a great struggle.

She died hard for one so beautiful, Gray Wolf thought, with an odd stirring of pity. He put his hand out to touch her cheek, which wasn't as cold as he had expected it to be. He moved his hand to her throat and pressed his fingers to the spot where, in the living, a pulse always throbbed. Feeling some faint movement there, Gray Wolf bent his ear to the swell of the woman's chest and heard a faint but unmistakable heartbeat.

When his hair brushed her face, the woman began to cough and make strangling sounds. Immediately Gray Wolf turned her over onto her stomach, locked his arms around her midsection, and pushed upward as hard as he could. The woman gagged and retched as a quantity of river water gushed from her mouth. Gray Wolf repeated the maneuver until all the water she had swallowed had left her stomach, and she struggled weakly to break free from his grasp.

As soon as Gray Wolf let her go, the woman sat up and began to shiver uncontrollably. He went to the canoe and returned in a moment with a warm woolen cloak he had found near the fish-hold.

He handed it to her, but then snatched it back when she tried to put it on over her wet dress. "You die if you stay in that," he said in English.

She looked as if she wanted to speak, then thought better of it and stood, making it clear by her gestures that she wanted something more from the canoe. He stood aside and let her go to it. She took a bundle of clothing and motioned toward a stand of thick bushes near the shore.

Interpreting her meaning, Gray Wolf almost smiled, something he rarely did, and gestured toward the canoe. "I busy here. I not follow you."

The woman regarded him briefly with her dark eyes, then turned and slowly made her way out of his sight.

As he unloaded the canoe, Gray Wolf realized he had probably been foolish to let the woman out of his sight. Suppose she didn't come back? Although obviously weak from her ordeal, she must be strong, or she'd never have been able to swim from the flatboat, fully clad, in such icy water. Why had they not seen her in the water? If they had, she surely would have died on the spot.

Gray Wolf uneasily remembered Black Oak's words. *You will*

take no prisoners. They scarcely had food for themselves, much less anyone else, so if she didn't return it would probably be for the best. Yet for some reason he could not put a name to, Gray Wolf believed this woman might turn out to be special.

I will find out who she really is, he promised himself. *Perhaps she might even be worth a fine ransom.*

❧

Susannah had no recollection of reaching the shore or of giving herself up to the welcome earth. The first thing she knew, something had an iron grip on her stomach, causing her to cough and retch and splutter until she had nothing more left to expel. The next thing she knew, she was staring into the face of the strangest man she had ever seen in her life.

This is a dream. It isn't real, Susannah thought at first, but the shivers that immediately began to wrack her body told her otherwise.

To begin with, the man dressed like an Indian, looked like an Indian, even smelled like an Indian—but Susannah had never known any Indian to have blue eyes and light brown hair. In profile, his straight, high-bridged nose and prominent cheekbones looked Indian-like, but there was no doubt that his skin, while tanned by years of exposure to the elements, was still probably whiter than her own.

When he saw her shivering, he went to the canoe and brought back a cloak she recognized as the one she had abandoned when she went into the water. She reached for it, eager to press its warmth to her wet body. But he took it away and spoke in English.

"You die in that."

Susannah started to speak, then decided it would be better not to engage this strange semi-Indian in any more conversation than was absolutely necessary. She stood, somewhat shakily, and went to the canoe, where she soon found her other clothes, still tied in a bundle. Susannah pointed to herself and then toward a thicket of bushes a few feet away. A final gesture of her hand told him not to follow her, an idea which he apparently found humorous.

"I busy here—I not follow you," he said in his strangely accented English, and turned his back to continue unloading the Hunters' goods.

This man and his companions killed them all, and he probably means to kill me, too, she realized. *I nearly drowned, only to reach the Indian side of the Ohio.* Her gait somewhat unsteady, Susannah walked away from him, half-expecting to feel the stab of an arrow in her back as she did so. *But why would he have brought me the cloak if he means to kill me?*

Susannah abandoned trying to puzzle it out; she was far too numbed from the cold to think clearly. She stripped off her sodden garments and shivered as she put on the welcome dry clothing. She left her mother's cross around her neck, and while the rawhide strand from which it hung was still damp, the wood felt almost warm on her skin. The gold coins remained safely in the waistband of her petticoat, which was too clammy to keep on. Susannah wrung as much water from her wet clothes as she could, then bundled them and came back to find that the man had started a small fire.

That's a good sign, she thought. Under the circumstances, Indian raiders wouldn't normally stop to warm themselves but would press on to wherever they'd come from. Susannah glanced at the waters of the Ohio River, gray now in the sunless morning light, and noted that the smoke from the burned flatboat had all but subsided. If anyone on the Kentucky side had seen it and come to investigate, perhaps they would also notice his fire on the far shore and rescue her.

However, even as she thought it, Susannah knew it was unlikely that anyone would come after her, at least not this soon. Even if they did, they would put her into fresh jeopardy; Indians never hesitated to kill their captives, especially if their presence might endanger them.

The man watched Susannah as she looked at the flatboat. He studied her face for what seemed a long time before he spoke again. "You not *schwannack.* Why you on boat?"

"My father is white, my man is white," she said. "I am called Susannah. What is your name?"

He turned his head to one side and looked at her as if trying to understand what she had said. "Su-sannah?" He touched his chest. "I Gray Wolf," he said.

"You look white" she said. "I think you have white parents."

Gray Wolf's frown wrinkled the bands of war paint on his brow. "I am Gray Wolf, son of the great Chief Black Oak." He pointed toward the ruins of the flatboat. "Your man there?" he asked.

Susannah shook her head. "No." She held out her left hand, displaying the thin band of gold she had worn for years. "My man is a mighty warrior who waits for me just up the river. He will come for me soon."

Gray Wolf folded his arms across his chest and raised his eyebrows, a clear indication that he didn't believe her. "But he not find you here," he said.

"Many armed warriors will come. If you don't want to bring your people trouble, leave me and go on your way. No one will follow you."

"My people have no word for one who does not speak true, but the *schwannack* would say you lie," he said calmly.

Almost automatically Susannah's hand groped for the wooden cross around her neck, and for the first time, Gray Wolf took notice of it.

I don't lie, Susannah wanted to say, but at the moment that would be an even greater falsehood. "Believe me or not, as you like. You will see," she said as calmly as she could.

Gray Wolf took a step forward, jerked Susannah's hand aside, and held the cross in his palm. "You think this piece of wood keep you safe?" he asked.

"No. It is the sign of a believer in Christ," Susannah replied.

Gray Wolf's expression grew stony and he stepped away from Susannah. "You pray to this wood?" he asked.

I have not prayed enough lately, she thought. "Not to the wood," she said. "We pray but to God."

"You waste breath. No one hears. No one answers," he said flatly.

He sounds bitter, Susannah thought, and guessed at a possible cause. "You know about Christ, don't you?"

Gray Wolf's blue eyes met hers, and for a brief moment he allowed her to see the sadness there before he looked away. "Once I believe," he said. "But not now. Not for long time."

"That must have been before you came to live with the Indians," Susannah said, but Gray Wolf had already turned away from her.

"Warm yourself now. Soon we go," he said.

"I will stay here," Susannah said.

Gray Wolf whirled around to face her, his face angry as he made the cut-off sign. "No! I say you go with me."

"What will you do with me?" Susannah asked, half-dreading his answer.

"Black Oak will say. But you not tell him about your man. He not like that."

"Why not?" Susannah asked, but Gray Wolf had evidently decided to say no more, and he returned to his tasks without another word.

Stretching her hands to the fire, Susannah thought about what might lie ahead for her. She had been only half-serious about wanting to stay on the shore. While someone might see and rescue her, it wasn't likely, and she knew her chances of surviving in Indian Territory, alone and in winter, were slim to none. On the other hand, she at least had some chance to live if Gray Wolf's people turned out to be kind.

Susannah had grown up hearing stories of how various groups of Indians had treated captives, those from other tribes as well as whites. Sometimes they were tortured, then killed. Some prisoners were allowed to live as slaves, while others married into the tribe and were left alone. Occasionally, captives were adopted as replacements for Indians who had been killed, and these individuals were treated as if they'd been born into the tribe.

That must be the case with Gray Wolf, Susannah thought as she watched him load the last of the goods onto the pack animals he'd tied in the woods while they raided the flatboat. There was no doubt in her mind that, whether or not he himself was fully aware of it, the man who called himself Gray Wolf had been born to two white parents. But in everything but his appearance, he seemed to be all Indian. Perhaps this Black Oak, the chief he called his father, might also be inclined to treat her kindly.

In any case, as Gray Wolf smothered the fire and signaled for Susannah to walk beside him, she found herself curious to see Gray Wolf's people and to find out how a white man had become a Woodlands Indian who could kill whites without a second thought.

four

A few hundred feet from shore, Gray Wolf stopped and waited for his companions to join him. Their eyes widened in surprise when they saw Susannah, and when they spoke, her heart beat faster as she recognized a few Delaware words.

These Indians must be either Delaware or a from closely related tribe, she realized. Many Woodlands Indians could speak Delaware, but they would not likely do so among their own kind if they shared a different language.

"Where did you get this woman?" the tallest Indian asked. Another, much shorter one, seemed angry.

"Why does this one still live? Black Oak said—"

"Sehe!" Gray Wolf cried. "This woman is not your concern. Go on your way."

"She does not look *schwannack*," the tall man said, but either Gray Wolf hadn't heard or had chosen to take no notice of his question, and the men said no more.

"They seem angry," Susannah said in English after the others were a considerable distance ahead. She didn't want Gray Wolf to know that she understood their words, but their expressions and the tone of their voices had made their feelings perfectly clear.

Gray Wolf did not look at her. "Do not speak," he said. "At village is better to be silent. When you see Black Oak, remember this."

"Does he speak English, too?" she asked.

"No. I speak for him," Gray Wolf said. "Now no more talk."

"But you haven't told me anything about yourself," Susannah said, making a final attempt to draw out this strange white

Indian.

Gray Wolf stopped in his tracks and turned to face Susannah. "No more talk," he repeated. "No—more—talk."

Despite the gravity of her situation, Gray Wolf's solemn admonition made Susannah feel an almost irresistible urge to giggle, which the look in his eyes promptly stifled.

Susannah and Gray Wolf walked on in silence, each wrapped in thoughts that the other couldn't begin to comprehend.

ᘑ

They emerged from a wooded area into an open meadow just as a pale sun broke through the clouds and began to cast shadows. Since they had traveled due north from the river and the shadows fell slightly to their right, Susannah knew it must be early afternoon. She hadn't eaten all day, nor had she thought about food until she smelled wood smoke and the tantalizing aroma of meat roasting over coals.

"We have game," Gray Wolf said, more to himself than her, and Susannah made no reply.

A few steps more brought them to a clearing where a dozen lodges stood in a rectangle, in the Delaware way. Several small cooking fires dotted the area. A half-grown boy tended a spitted rabbit. Over another fire was set an iron cooking pot in which stew bubbled, and underneath it, tubers roasted in the ashes.

"We saw you coming and made ready," the boy tending the rabbit said to Gray Wolf.

"You did well," Gray Wolf told him. "We have fasted these two days."

They won't eat yet, though. The thought came to Susannah instinctively, although she did not know why.

She looked around at the dwellings, at the women busy with their tasks, at the sleeping babies who lay in cradleboards on their mothers' back, and felt a strange sense that she had been here before, that she knew these people.

It is the way Mother described her village on the

Monongahela—that must be the reason I feel I know it already, Susannah told herself. She had never seen an Indian village, nor had she ever been this far into Indian Territory. But her father had probably long-hunted in these parts many times over the years. He'd met many Indians before he'd fallen in love with her mother, the lovely Sukeu-quawon, a Delaware maiden who had shot him with an arrow, mistaking him for a deer.

Susannah half-smiled, thinking of the relish with which her father always told the story. Then someone spoke sharply, rousing her from the odd mood the sight of the camp had created.

"You! Come over here!" a woman called out in Delaware.

Susannah blinked and looked at the apparition before her in disbelief. The speaker was a woman who might once have been tall, but was now bent, with a shock of white hair that hung over her squinted eyes and wrinkled face. She was toothless, or nearly so, and wore such filthy rags that it was hard to know what they once might have been. Over her shoulders hung a massive buffalo robe, so moth-eaten and tattered that Susannah doubted it could possibly furnish much warmth. With a final inviting crook of her finger, the woman turned away and went into a lodge, leaving Susannah uncertain of what she should do.

Gray Wolf had been supervising unloading the packhorses, a procedure that had attracted many willing hands, but now he turned and approached Susannah. "Go with Dark Moon. I come for you when it is time," he said.

"Who is Dark Moon?" Susannah asked, but Gray Wolf had already walked away.

I guess I'll have to find out for myself, she thought as she bent to enter the strange old woman's lodge.

Immediately a number of sensations assailed Susannah, and it took her a while to sort them out. For one thing, the lodge was dark. Only the entrance, covered with a deerskin to keep out the cold, and the smoke-hole in the roof admitted any light. The fire that always burned in the lodge had been banked to ashes but still radiated heat. On the walls hung animal skins in all stages of preparation, from the rank one near the door, obviously freshly killed, to others that had been tanned and worked smooth. The smell of the fire and the hides and the ever-present odor of bear grease were part of what Susannah had always thought of as Indian smells. Neither pleasant or unpleasant, but somehow familiar—what she would have expected to find in a Delaware lodge.

However, the one Gray Wolf had called Dark Moon was unlike any old woman Susannah had ever seen, Indian or white, and when she came forward and put her hands on Susannah's face, it was all she could do to stand quietly and not break and run away.

Dark Moon stroked Susannah's cheeks and chin, then felt her hair and clasped her hands. "Ahh," the woman said. "Is it Fair Star come back to me?"

"I am called Susannah," Susannah said in English, but the woman gave no sign that she understood. She took the bundle of damp clothes Susannah still carried and backed away with it. She unwrapped it and ran her hands over the material of the dress and petticoats. Then Dark Moon fell to her knees and began rummaging among the heaped blankets and skins on the lodge floor.

Her eyesight must be failing, Susannah thought. She resolved to retrieve her petticoat as soon as she could, before Dark Moon found the gold coins hidden in it. Dark Moon continued to grope around until her hands encountered a deerskin shift, which she thrust at Susannah.

"Do you give me this?" Susannah asked in Delaware.

In reply, the woman laughed, an eerie sound that set Susannah's nerves on edge. "Ahh—ee, Fair Star," she said, then repeated the words until they became a kind of chant.

Dark Moon sat cross-legged, her eyes closed, alternately laughing and chanting, as if she had forgotten that Susannah existed.

She must be mad, Susannah guessed. Her mother had told her that the Lenni-Lenape had special regard for the insane and always cared for them tenderly, no matter how strange their behavior.

Susannah briefly debated if she should exchange her homespun dress for the deerskin shift, then decided against it. If Gray Wolf wanted her to change clothes before he took her to the chief, he would tell her.

Susannah shook her head as she realized that she already expected the strange white Indian to tell her what to do, just as James always had. But her husband was dead, and she had chosen not to depend on Nate McIntyre's offer of protection. *I surely don't intend to turn my life over to Gray Wolf,* Susannah reminded herself.

Tired and hungry and not knowing how long it might be before Chief Black Oak called for her, Susannah lay down on a soft bearskin, pulled up a blanket, and fell into a light sleep.

❧

Susannah awoke to find Dark Moon bending over and shaking her. She sat up, at first unsure why she was being awakened. Then she saw Gray Wolf holding aside the door-flap, apparently waiting for her.

"Black Oak see you now," he said.

Susannah attempted to smooth her hair, which she had worn unbraided ever since the drunken man in Lexington had called her a squaw, a scene that unaccountably came to her mind as she followed Gray Wolf toward the largest lodge, the one she had already guessed must be the chief's.

"I'm hungry," she said, noting that whatever had been cooking when they'd reached the village had either been eaten or taken somewhere else.

"*Schwannack* always hungry," Gray Wolf said. "You eat later."

"I hope so," Susannah said. Although she thought she had regained her strength following the loss of her baby, there were times when she still felt a bit weak, particularly when she hadn't eaten for several hours.

"You no talk," Gray Wolf reminded her as he took her arm and led her into the chief's presence.

The lodge where the chief and his elders sat in a half circle was both larger and brighter than Dark Moon's. Susannah noted the trenchers stacked in one corner and hoped that meant that food might be served soon.

Gray Wolf bowed before Black Oak, and Susannah did likewise. The chief rose from his seat and slowly walked toward, then completely around Susannah. His inspection reminded her of the way her Uncle Joshua examined a horse or cow he was thinking of buying, and it was hard for her to stand still.

With no change in his expression, Black Oak returned to his seat. "I say no prisoners," Black Oak told Gray Wolf in Delaware. "Why does this one live?"

Gray Wolf glanced at Susannah, then back to Black Oak. "Can you not see, Father? This one is not *schwannack.* She is called Su-sannah."

"She was on the *schwannack* boat?" Black Oak asked.

Gray Wolf shifted his weight from one foot to the other. "I do not see her there. I find her on the shore."

Black Oak frowned. "She came from the boat." It was a statement that Gray Wolf made no effort to deny. "She may be *schujipaw.*"

The Delaware word was not familiar to Susannah, but from the way it had been spoken, she guessed that Black Oak thought she might be a spy.

"I do not think this is so, Father."

Black Oak leaned forward and pointed to the ring on

Susannah's left hand. "What about her man?"

"She says she has no man," Gray Wolf said, and it was all Susannah could do to keep from challenging him. But to do so would also let them know that she understood Delaware, and she wasn't yet ready to do that.

"I see why you bring her here," Black Oak said. "It has been a long year."

"It is not so, Father," Gray Wolf protested, but Black Oak appeared not to hear him and raised his hand in dismissal.

"The council will consider what to do about this woman— and your disobedience. Go and break your fast."

Gray Wolf struck his chest with his fist and turned to Susannah, who had deliberately made no move to leave. "Come, you eat now," he said.

Susannah nodded to Black Oak and followed Gray Wolf out of the lodge.

"Go back to Dark Moon," Gray Wolf directed. "I send you food."

"What did Black Oak say?" Susannah asked at the entrance to Dark Moon's lodge.

He shrugged. "Nothing. Black Oak talks, elders talk. You know soon."

Gray Wolf turned away, but before she went inside, Susannah called after him. "I do have a man," she said, but he walked on, giving no indication that he had even heard her.

Susannah ducked into the lodge, nettled that Gray Wolf hadn't responded to her parting words and wondering why she cared.

≈

Under the watchful eyes of Dark Moon, who laughed mirthlessly from time to time, Susannah ate all the food a shy young maid had brought her. From the nut-flavored soup and savory stew to the crisp, black leg of rabbit and roasted tuber, everything tasted delicious. She drank deeply from the jug of spring water that accompanied the food, then, sated, she sat back to wait to be summoned again into Black Oak's presence.

Reviewing their brief encounter, Susannah thought about the man that Gray Wolf called "Father." Although it was obvious that he wasn't accustomed to having his orders disobeyed, Black Oak didn't look fierce or seem to be unreasonable. Perhaps if she found favor with him, he might agree to send her back across the Ohio. Susannah knew that was the best she could hope for; the worst, that he would order her to be put to death, she thought quite unlikely. Still, one way or another, at this moment, her future depended on the chief's decision.

It will be Black Oak's alone, Susannah thought, despite what both he and Gray Wolf had said to the contrary. The chief had to have the consent of his warriors before taking them into battle, but in other matters, the Delaware village chiefs generally ordered what was to be done. That was the Delaware way.

Maybe I should have spoken Delaware to him, after all, she thought. But not all the Lenni-Lenape were on friendly terms, and since Black Oak might already suspect her of being a spy, she had probably done well to say nothing.

It is so hard to know what to do. As Susannah often did in times of stress, she found herself stroking her mother's cross. An image came to her mind of her mother kneeling in prayer with her children around her, the cross always around her neck as a symbol of her faith. *I wish I could pray with my mother's trust,* Susannah thought.

But it had been many years since Susannah had heard her mother's prayers, and for some time her own petitions hardly seemed strong enough to reach the treetops, much less be heard all the way to heaven.

Help me, God, Susannah prayed. Her request might not be very specific, but if God listened at all, Susannah believed He would surely know how to help her.

❧

Twenty-four hours after she had awakened on the flatboat, Susannah once more heard a noise that she didn't associate with her surroundings and instantly awoke.

Dark Moon still slept. The heavy breathing that had bordered into snoring many times through the night was the only sound in the lodge, but from outside came shouting voices, too far away for any words to be clear. From the general tone, however, Susannah guessed that someone had sounded an alarm, and her heart began to beat more rapidly.

Could someone have followed Gray Wolf here to avenge his attack on the flatboat?

Susannah knew it wasn't likely, but when she went to the doorway and raised the flap to look out, she half-hoped to see a party of white frontiersmen coming to her rescue. However, the shouting came from a single Indian, perhaps a scout sent out by Black Oak or a messenger from another village.

"We must leave in haste," a familiar voice called out, and soon Gray Wolf came into the clearing, followed by a growing band of armed warriors who seemed to be both ready and eager to do battle.

Knowing that Gray Wolf had probably forgotten all about her in the excitement, Susannah left Dark Moon's lodge and followed him to the edge of the village, where the village's precious horses were kept corralled. "What is happening?" she asked.

Gray Wolf turned and frowned at Susannah. "It does not concern you," he said. "Stay with Dark Moon."

"If you go to Kentucky, take me with you," she said.

Gray Wolf laughed without humor. "You and Dark Moon good company," he said, implying that her request was insane.

"When will you be back?" she asked.

Gray Wolf pointed to the lodge she had just left and half pushed her toward it. "Stay inside," Gray Wolf said. "This not matter for women."

Reluctantly Susannah started back to Dark Moon's, aware that she was the only female in sight. She stood in the lodge entrance and watched as the village men left, heading west.

The instant the men disappeared from sight, women began coming out of their lodges. They stopped in the center of the village and waited as one of their number, a tall woman with regal bearing, walked over to Susannah and motioned for her to join them.

Something about their expressions frightened Susannah, and their absolute silence as she walked toward them and stood in their midst was more chilling than the harshest words would have been.

"This one wears fine *schwannack* clothes," someone said loudly.

"Ay-ee, and gold," another said.

Susannah wanted to turn and run away from them, but she knew the Delaware women would have only contempt for her if she showed the slightest sign of fear. Slowly Susannah removed her ring and held it out to the woman who had spoken last.

"Do you want this?" she asked in Delaware.

There was a silence, then a low murmuring as they turned to one another, speaking of this *schwannack* woman who not only resembled them, but also spoke their tongue.

"We take it," the first woman said, and advanced on her.

"Perhaps we should wait to see what Black Oak will do," one of the younger women suggested timidly, but already Susannah had been surrounded. A quick hand snatched the cross from her neck, then others surged forward and began to remove her clothing, piece by piece, until she stood shivering in cold and humiliation.

"Why do you do this?" Susannah tried to ask, but no one would answer her.

Susannah hugged her arms across her chest and wished that

the earth would open and take her away from this place, or that she had drowned in the Ohio River and gotten it over with.

Why are such terrible things happening to me, Lord? What have I ever done to deserve such treatment?

"What will we do with this one?" one woman asked.

"We take her to the woods and leave her," the tall woman said.

Susannah raised her head and looked at her tormentors. The village that had seemed like an old and familiar place only a few hours before was now cold and entirely alien, and she knew it wouldn't matter what Black Oak decided to do with her—if they left her alone in the woods she would die of the cold in only a matter of hours unless someone helped her. Yet from the expressions on their faces, the women apparently were unmoved by her predicament.

I will not plead for my life, Susannah thought, knowing that would be the surest way to lose it.

"Help me take her." The tall woman stepped forward and took hold of one of Susannah's arms, and a woman with a baby in a cradleboard took the other.

Before they could take a step, however, an awful scream rent the air, and the women shrank back as Dark Moon emerged from her lodge with the longest knife Susannah had ever seen held high in her hand.

"Leave her alone!" Dark Moon cried, and the women scattered before her advance as quickly as autumn leaves before a windstorm.

Susannah didn't wait for an invitation to run into the warmth and privacy of Dark Moon's lodge, nor did she hesitate to cover her cold body with the deerskin garment that the woman had offered her the day before. When she realized that Dark Moon hadn't followed her into the lodge. Susannah took advantage of her absence to insure that the gold coins still rested undisturbed in the waistband of her spare petticoat.

I must find a better way to hide them, she thought. If she tore a strip of cloth from the bottom of her petticoat, she could wrap the coins in it and tie it around her waist. Someday, if she could only keep them, those coins might save her life.

Susannah searched unsuccessfully for something sharp to help her start a tear in the petticoat, then stopped and stood still when she realized that Dark Moon had returned.

The woman filled the doorway of the lodge, breathing heavily and muttering under her breath. She still held the knife, and Susannah saw with relief that it didn't appear to have been used. On her little finger she now wore Susannah's gold wedding band, and around her neck was Susannah's wooden cross.

Susannah wet her lips and sought the right words to say. "Thank you for helping me," she said in Delaware.

Dark Moon grunted and peered at Susannah through a screen of wild white hair. "Fair Star? You come back?" She held out her arms and started toward Susannah, who instinctively backed away.

"I am not Fair Star," Susannah said in English. To her consternation, the old woman bowed her head and began to wail and beat her breast in the Lenni-Lenape way of mourning.

"All gone," Dark Moon said in English. "My man. My babies. Fair Star. All gone." She raised her head and glared at Susannah, then elevated the hand that held the knife and stepped forward until its tip almost touched Susannah's throat.

Her breath nearly stopped with fear, Susannah stood still and struggled for composure. "You have had a hard life," she said in English, then repeated in Delaware.

Dark Moon threw her head back and laughed in a way that sent cold chills down Susannah's back. "Ay-eee, ay-eee."

"I am sorry for your pain," Susannah said, but the old woman no longer seemed to notice her. Dark Moon collapsed into a heap and began to sob raggedly, hugging her body with her arms and rocking back and forth, with the knife still firmly clutched in her hand.

Susannah backed away, sat down on the other side of the fire, and wondered how safe she really was in this strange woman's lodge. The few words Dark Moon had spoken in English convinced Susannah that the woman might be, like herself, at least partly white. But who was Fair Star, and why did the old woman keep calling Susannah by that name?

I wish I could talk to her, Susannah thought, but she feared that Dark Moon was incapable of carrying on any real conversation.

Eventually Dark Moon's sobs subsided to whimpers, and then to even breathing as she slept. When the knife fell from her relaxed hand, Susannah retrieved it and hid it as well as she could by sticking it into the frame of the lodge near the doorway and underneath a tanning skin. Then she opened the door-flap enough to look out and saw that the village women had resumed their ordinary tasks. No one looked her way, but Susannah feared what they might do if she went out among them again, and she put the flap down and retreated to the far end of Dark Moon's lodge.

With a lovely tortoise-shell comb she found among a jumble of wampum and shells, Susannah combed the tangles from her hair and braided it. She tied the ends with strips of rawhide she took from a bundle of dried herbs. Their pungent odor reminded Susannah of the store of dried plants her mother had used to treat a variety of ills as well as to make their house smell fresh, and she felt a renewed sense of loss.

My mother could never have had such fond memories of her childhood if she'd lived in a village like this, Susannah decided. No, these people, whoever they were, were definitely not the gentle Lenni-Lenape that Sukeu-quawon had spoken of with such pride to Susannah and her brothers and sisters.

"Never forget that the blood of the brave Delaware people

runs in your veins, too," she had told her children. "It is a proud thing to know."

I am not proud now, Susannah thought. *I am white. I am not any part of these Indians.*

The deerskin shift, while shapeless and not quite long enough to cover her ankles, was comfortable, and since the village women would probably take her other homespun dress, anyway, it wouldn't be wise to garb herself as a *schwannack.* To keep her legs warm, Susannah wrapped them in strips of deerskin and worked her feet into a pair of Dark Moon's worn moccasins.

I am white, not Indian, Susannah had declared. Yet dressed as she was and with her glossy black hair in braids, Susannah had no idea just how much like Sukeu-quawon she really looked.

five

Several times in the next two days Susannah tried in both English and Delaware to engage Dark Moon in conversation, but without success. The old woman shared food with her, but otherwise it was as if Susannah just did not exist.

On the morning of the third day after the village men had left, Dark Moon opened the door-flap and peered out, sniffing the frosty air as if scenting something on the wind. "They should be back by now," she said distinctly in English.

Surprised, Susannah took a moment to consider how she should respond. "Do you know where they went?" she asked.

Dark Moon turned and laughed in the mirthless way that always set Susannah on edge. "They go where there is trouble," she said. Although she spoke in English, her speech was accented in the cadences of the Delaware language, much as Susannah's own mother's had been.

"How long have you lived in this village?" Susannah asked.

The old woman touched the cross, which she had worn around her neck constantly since taking it from Susannah's tormentors, and groaned as if remembering something too terrible to utter. "This village is new," she said. "No one lives here before."

From the construction of the lodges and the condition of the grounds around them, Susannah had already guessed that Black Oak's people had only recently moved there, but Dark Moon's ambiguous reply revealed nothing about her own past, and Susannah tried again. "How long have you been with these people?"

Dark Moon squinted as if trying to see Susannah better. "I

was young then, younger than you now." She spoke softly, and Susannah leaned forward in an attempt to hear her better.

"What brought you here?" Susannah asked.

The light of understanding that had flickered briefly in Dark Moon's eyes seemed to dim, then went out completely as deep, wrenching sobs shook her large frame.

Whatever happened to her must have been too horrible to recall, Susannah realized. Impulsively she hugged the old woman. Immediately Dark Moon pulled away and ran shrieking out of the lodge. When she returned a few minutes later, it was as if she had never before spoken to, or even seen Susannah.

Yet from time to time the rest of that morning, Susannah noticed Dark Moon looking at her and muttering to herself, and she wondered if the crazed woman might be planning to do her some harm. Then another thought became a full-blown suspicion. *Perhaps Dark Moon isn't really as crazy as she wants to appear to be.* The woman definitely had periods of rationality, and looking back on it, Susannah thought that Dark Moon's dramatic knife-wielding might have been at least partially faked. As long as Susannah and the village women feared her, the old woman had power over them.

In the midst of such thoughts, Susannah didn't notice the commotion outside until Dark Moon sprang to her feet and opened the door-flap. Susannah joined her and peered out to see a few children running toward the first of the returning village men.

"The boy comes back," Dark Moon muttered.

Unsure of what she had said, Susannah stared at her. "The boy?"

As if she hadn't heard her, Dark Moon took a few steps away from the lodge and waited for the only blue-eyed, blond Indian among the returning warriors to greet her.

Susannah's head whirled as she considered the possibility that Dark Moon and Gray Wolf were mother and son. If so, it would explain some things she had wondered about, while raising even more questions. Susannah wished she could hear what they were saying, but she was too far away. After a moment, Dark Moon turned and pointed to Susannah, who still stood in the lodge doorway. Gray Wolf glanced at her, then back at Dark Moon, then back at Susannah as if he doubted his eyes.

He hasn't seen me wearing Indian dress before, Susannah realized. *That must be the reason for the strange way he's looking at me.*

Thinking Gray Wolf would surely come and speak to her, Susannah stood by the lodge door and waited. However, Gray Wolf returned his attention to the laden packhorses without another glance in her direction. With a chill, Susannah realized that the men must have been raiding again, and from the amount of goods they had brought back, it had more likely been a whole settlement rather than just a flatboat that was attacked. Unloading and distributing the skins and food would take some time, so it was unlikely she would see Gray Wolf for several hours.

Oddly disappointed, Susannah went back into the lodge and sat down. By now, Black Oak must surely have decided what to do with her. Maybe he'd already confided his decision to Gray Wolf and he was avoiding her because he knew that she would be put to death.

Stop it! Susannah admonished herself. One of the Bible verses her family quoted most often, "Sufficient unto the day is the evil thereof," was sometimes shortened to, "Don't borrow trouble." People who had a great deal of anxiety about the future never found happiness in the present.

True enough, Susannah thought, *but only as long as there is a tomorrow to look forward to.*

When Dark Moon returned to the lodge some time later, Susannah again asked her if Gray Wolf was her son, but she pretended not to hear. *I will ask him myself when I see him,*

Susannah decided and hoped it would be soon.

❧

Gray Wolf did not like to be distracted when he was raiding, yet all the while he was away from her, he found himself thinking of the beautiful woman called Su-sannah, who looked so strangely Delaware.

I was wrong to bring her to the village, he told himself many times, but in his heart he knew that, had he to live the day of the flatboat raid over, he would do the same thing. He hadn't believed her story that her man would find her if he left her on the Ohio shore, nor did he believe that anyone would seek her in Indian Territory. However, traders often brought ransom offers from whites whose relatives were among the Indians. Gray Wolf had reminded Black Oak of that possibility when, as they were riding back from the raid, her fate was mentioned.

"I know you have some other interest in this woman," Black Oak had said, and although Gray Wolf had angrily denied it, such an interest did exist. But she was from the whites, and Gray Wolf had sworn an oath of enmity to all whites when he was a child, on the most terrible day of his young life—

"I know she is not a spy," Gray Wolf had said. "Deal with her as you will."

They had not spoken of the matter again, and by the time they rode back into the village, Gray Wolf had half-convinced himself that he didn't care what Black Oak did about her. Yet when Dark Moon came out to greet him and he saw Su-sannah again, the sight took his breath away.

Wearing deerskin and moccasins and with her hair in braids, the woman would easily pass as a full-blooded Delaware, at least at first glance.

Seeing him look at Susannah, Dark Moon spoke words that shocked him to the core. "The woman speaks and understands some Delaware. She must have lived among the Lenni-Lenape before."

"Surely this is not so, old woman," Gray Wolf said. Dark Moon often slipped into periods of madness in which she might say or do anything. But this day the light of reason shone in her eyes, and he did not doubt that she thought she spoke the truth.

He looked again at Su-sannah, anger overcoming his initial thrill of pleasure on seeing her. *The woman could understand what we said all the time.* Why hadn't she let him know?

Maybe she is a spy, after all, he thought as he turned away. *Black Oak can do with her as he will—I want no more to do with this woman.*

Gray Wolf's mind readily made the vow, but his heart did not fully agree.

&

It was late in the afternoon when Dappled Faun, the shy young maiden who often brought food to Susannah and Dark Moon, came to summon Susannah to Black Oak's lodge.

"Will you come with me?" she asked Dark Moon, but the old woman merely muttered something unintelligible and turned away. Susannah touched her neck as if her cross still hung there and wished she knew what to pray for as she followed Dappled Faun to Black Oak's lodge.

May God give me strength to bear what I must, Susannah murmured.

The moment she stepped inside the lodge, Susannah sensed an atmosphere of celebration, and her heart lifted. All things considered, she could do much worse than to be brought before a council in a festive mood.

Gray Wolf was seated at Black Oak's right hand. He barely glanced at her when she half-bowed to the chief.

Black Oak's dark eyes regarded her steadily before he spoke in Delaware. "You call yourself Su-sannah. You come from *schwannack* boat. You know our tongue yet you do not speak it to us. Why is this so?"

The chief's words took her by surprise. *Someone who heard me speaking Delaware must have told him,* she realized. It could have been one of the village women, but she suspected it more likely that Dark Moon had told him.

Susannah glanced at Gray Wolf, who sat with his arms folded across his chest, his expression impassive. Her heart sank as she realized that Gray Wolf must already know it, too. *He will not help me now,* she realized, and wondered why that knowledge was so painful to bear.

Looking back at Black Oak, Susannah raised her hands, palms up, in the ancient gesture of supplication and took a deep breath. "I was told not to speak in your presence. I do not mean to wrong you, *muchomes.*"

Black Oak frowned. "I will not ask who told you such a thing. You come from the *schwannack,* yet in our dress, you are as one of us." He turned to Gray Wolf and said something else, but he spoke so rapidly that Susannah could make out only a few words.

"I do not understand all you say, mighty Chief," Susannah said earnestly when Black Oak stopped speaking and looked at her as if expecting her to speak on her behalf. "I am the daughter of Sukeu-quawon, of the People of the Serpent on the Monongahela River. My father is a mighty hunter called Jonathan McKay. He is a friend to the Lenni-Lenape. I live far away, in the land of my father's people."

Black Oak conferred with the other council members in low tones, then turned back to Susannah. "We do not know this man McKay, and the Clan of the Serpent is no longer by the Monongahela. Many enemies seek to harm us. It might be that you have been sent by them."

Susannah looked steadily at Black Oak and hoped that he could detect the sincerity in her voice. "It is not so, Chief. I am no enemy of Black Oak or his people."

Black Oak looked directly at Gray Wolf. "You brought this

woman here. She is your captive. What will you have done with her?"

Gray Wolf heard the chief's words with the same maddening impassivity that he had shown earlier. "You are the chief, my father. The woman has told you who she is. You must do with her what you will."

Black Oak nodded as if something had been settled. "Go now. We feast tonight," he said.

"Thank you, *muchomes*," Susannah murmured, unsure of what he had done that required her thanks, but knowing it to be the polite way to end the strange interview. She turned and left the lodge, half-hoping that Gray Wolf might follow her and explain what had just happened. But he didn't, and under the watchful eyes of Dark Moon, Susannah settled down to wait for nightfall and the feast of celebration, when she expected to learn her fate.

☙

In addition to goods and pelts, the men had returned with freshly-killed game, and all day the women busied themselves gathering wood for the many fires over which the meat cooked. It was well after sunset when the villagers began crowding into Black Oak's lodge for the dancing and chanting that would precede the feast.

Dark Moon's eyes glittered with excitement as she entered the lodge with Susannah. She sat down by the door and began to sway her torso in time to the insistent beat of the drums, apparently enjoying herself.

The drums are like a heartbeat, Susannah thought, herself soon caught up in the steady rhythm of the dance. Around in a circle the men went, the shells on their arms and around their ankles faintly jingling as their bodies rose and bent in time to the drum. The women watched, most in silence. A few cast curious glances at Susannah, but whatever fury had seized them the day they had taken her clothes seemed to have been cast aside, at least while they were in the chief's lodge.

Finally the dancing ended, and food was borne in on huge wooden slabs and distributed in a more or less orderly manner. Over the din, Black Oak motioned for Susannah to sit at his feet, an invitation that drew some notice from the other women. Although she didn't feel at all hungry, Susannah made sure that she took something from every dish offered to her. It wouldn't be mannerly to refuse anything, and Susannah certainly didn't want to insult the chief at this critical moment.

When the feasting was finished, Black Oak walked to the center of the lodge, stood in front of the fire, and raised his arms aloft as a signal that he was about to say something. As many as could seated themselves on the earthen floor, and the others stood around the lodge walls. All was silent as he began to speak.

Susannah's knowledge of Delaware didn't allow her to follow everything that Black Oak said. He began with an oration praising the bravery of the warriors who had raided their enemies—that much she understood, although she couldn't make out what he said about the location or identity of those enemies. By name he praised a half-dozen warriors, ending with his sons. After they had stood in turn and bowed to acknowledge Black Oak's praise, the chief motioned for Gray Wolf to come forward.

"Bring the woman here," Black Oak directed, and immediately Gray Wolf turned to Susannah, who quickly stood without aid, ignoring the hand he had extended to help her rise.

Her action sent a murmur through the villagers, and once more Susannah realized she must have unwittingly violated some tribal tradition.

Susannah and Gray Wolf stood facing Black Oak, who held a very long, very sharp knife in his raised hand. Its blade shone in the firelight as he began to chant, softly at first, and then more loudly.

For the first time that night, fear for her life gripped Susannah, and instinctively she touched her neck, groping for but not finding the comfort of her cross. *Lord, can it be Your will for my life to end here, after all?*

Still chanting, Black Oak reached for Susannah's left forearm. He turned it upward, exposing her palm, and almost before she had time to understand what was happening, he made a small incision in her wrist with the point of the knife. She felt a sharp sting as the blade broke her skin, immediately drawing blood. Then Black Oak turned to Gray Wolf and held the knife out to him. He shook his head, and the villagers gasped at his refusal.

Black Oak dropped Susannah's hand and seized Gray Wolf's, jabbing his wrist in the same place he had cut Susannah's. Almost as soon as the blood began to flow from the wound, Black Oak brought their wrists together and held them as the bright red blood from each mingled.

In an almost eerie silence, Black Oak raised their joined wrists. "I bind Gray Wolf and Su-sannah with blood," he said. He raised another brief chant before he lashed their wrists together with a rawhide thong. When he finished, Black Oak stepped back and raised his arms over them in what Susannah took to be a benediction of some sort. She looked down at her bloody wrist, then raised questioning eyes to Gray Wolf, who stared stonily ahead.

He doesn't like this any better than I do, Susannah thought, but at least Gray Wolf knew what the ritual meant.

No one spoke as Black Oak resumed his seat in the midst of the tribal council, whose impassive faces did not betray what they thought of the ceremony that had just taken place. "Go now, my son," Black Oak said.

A muscle worked in Gray Wolf's cheek, indicating that he was having a hard time keeping his anger in check. "We will speak more of this," he said shortly.

"It is done," Black Oak said forcefully. "I will hear no more talk."

Susannah winced as Gray Wolf turned suddenly. She struggled to match his long steps as he strode out of the lodge, their wrists still painfully bound. With the laughter of several village children trailing them, Gray Wolf walked in the silvery light of a full moon to his small lodge on the edge of the village.

"Do not move. I make better fire," Gray Wolf said.

Gingerly she knelt while he used his free right hand to kindle the ashes to flame, then added several small branches from a white oak.

"What does this mean?" Susannah asked in English, gesturing with her right hand toward their bound wrists.

Gray Wolf looked at Susannah as if he wanted to strike her. "You not tell me you speak Delaware," he said accusingly.

"You told me not to say anything, and I didn't," Susannah replied.

"I mean from the first," he said. "You knew we were Delaware."

Susannah looked away, uncomfortable under Gray Wolf's scrutiny. "After a time I did, but I feared for my life. I wanted to see what you intended to do with me. Besides, I do not understand all you say in Delaware."

Gray Wolf shook his head. "Running Fox was right," he said grimly.

Take no prisoners, the orders had been. Gray Wolf wished he had killed her, she supposed. But why was he so angry with her now?

"I do not mean to make things hard for you," she said.

Gray Wolf gave no response to her attempt at apology. "I take the binding away," he said steadily. "The blood will start again."

Susannah winced as Gray Wolf unwrapped the rawhide thong

and removed his wrist from hers. Their blood had clotted together, but now fresh blood seeped from the wrist of each. Gray Wolf turned aside and searched through a jumble of cloth until he found a few scraps of linen.

"You first," he said, wrapping the linen around her slowly seeping wound.

When it was her turn to bandage Gray Wolf's wrist, Susannah thought she detected a pale scar beside the new cut, but in the uncertain light of the fire it was hard to tell. Susannah felt almost certain that Gray Wolf had been through the ceremony with someone else, but his impassive expression suggested that he probably wouldn't tell her, even if she asked.

Susannah finished tucking the ends of the bandage around his wrist. "How does that feel?"

Gray Wolf held out his hand and flexed his fingers. "You did well," he said with a note of grudging surprise in his tone.

"There are healers in my family," Susannah said.

At the mention of her family, Gray Wolf looked at Susannah strangely. "You do not tell Black Oak about your man," he said. "Why is this?"

Susannah glanced at her ringless left hand. Gray Wolf's question reminded her how keenly she still felt the loss of her husband, but she was not ready to admit to Gray Wolf that she was a widow. "He did not ask. I thought you had told him."

"I tell Black Oak what I think is true. He is chief; he does what he likes."

"But you are his son. He listens to you."

Gray Wolf cocked his head in the way he had of seeming to test what Susannah was telling him, then he shrugged. "Sometimes this is so. Sometimes it is not." He walked to the door of his lodge and looked out. "I go now. The fire should last the night."

Without another word or a backward glance, Gray Wolf was gone, leaving Susannah to stare after him in surprise. Although

Gray Wolf hadn't said what the ceremony of binding meant, Susannah thought that it must mean that they were married, at least in the eyes of Black Oak and his people.

But not as James and I were married, in the eyes of God and because we loved one another. Susannah's eyes filled with tears as she thought of the vows she and James had exchanged, vows that bound them for only a few brief years. Susannah knew she would never again love anyone else the way she had loved James. As for the strange white Indian who called himself Gray Wolf—

He is no more eager to be bound to me than I am to marry him. A thought came to Susannah as a certainty. *He has been married, as well, and the woman's name was Fair Star.*

I'll ask Dark Moon about her, Susannah decided.

As if thinking of the woman had somehow summoned her, Dark Moon herself opened the door-flap and entered Gray Wolf's lodge. "Where is Gray Wolf?" she asked in her strangely-accented English, and Susannah felt relieved to see that the old woman seemed rational.

"I don't know," Susannah said.

Without invitation, Dark Moon sat beside Susannah and took her hand, examining the wrist that had been marked during the binding ceremony. "If he does not stay here with you, it is a disgrace," she said.

"Gray Wolf is your son, isn't he?" Susannah asked, seizing the opportunity to speak of something that she had long wondered about.

Dark Moon seemed not to have heard the question. "Other warriors will seek to have this binding," she said.

"I will have to choose another?" Susannah asked.

Dark Moon laughed, a deep chuckle that lacked humor. "You do not choose," the old woman told her. "I see Running Fox watch you. I know that one wants you."

Running Fox—the warrior from the flatboat raid who had

thought from the first that Susannah should be killed. Imagining how she would feel to be claimed as his wife, Susannah shuddered. "I will not allow it," she said, and once more Dark Moon laughed.

"It is not for you to say, Su-sannah. You should stay with your own people."

You don't know how I wish I had, Susannah thought. Changing the subject, Susannah asked another question. "Who is Fair Star? Do I look like her?"

Dark Moon's face crumpled, and she threw her head back in a keening cry that sent chills through Susannah's body. "Ay-eee," she cried, over and over again.

Whoever Fair Star was, Dark Moon must have loved her very much, Susannah realized.

"Come now," Susannah said when the woman's sobs had begun to subside. "We will go back to your lodge."

The old woman allowed Susannah to help her walk through the village, but at the door to her lodge she stopped and pressed Susannah's arm. "Running Fox must not find you here."

"Surely he will not look for me this night," Susannah said.

"He will look to see that Gray Wolf stays with you," Dark Moon said.

"What can I do, then?" Susannah asked when Dark Moon continued to block her entrance to the lodge.

"Leave this village," Dark Moon said. She leaned so close to Susannah that her hair brushed her forehead. "Once I had the chance to go, but I stayed. Your man not like it if you stay here."

"Will you let me have my things back if I go?" asked Susannah.

Dark Moon seemed to consider the question for a moment, then she opened the door-flap and motioned for Susannah to enter the lodge. In the dim light of the fire, she took the gold ring from her finger and handed it to Susannah. "You take this," she said. "I keep the other."

Susannah hesitated. The wedding band that James had placed on her finger still meant a great deal to her as a reminder of their love. But Susannah's attachment to the simple cross, which had almost no monetary value, went back many more years and was even more meaningful.

"The cross was my mother's," she said. "Keep the ring and give me the cross."

Dark Moon's fist closed around it, and she shook her head. "No."

"All right," Susannah agreed, seeing she had little choice. "I would like to take only one other thing I brought with me."

Dark Moon folded her arms across her chest and chuckled. "The gold coins? I keep those. You take the *schwannack* clothes. I also give you warm blanket."

Susannah wanted to shake this exasperating woman who, under guise of considering her welfare, had managed to rob Susannah of the most precious of her meager possessions. She tried to make her voice calm as she pointed out, "You have no use for the coins."

"Neither will you when you find your people."

"It will not be an easy journey," Susannah said. "It is a long way back to the river, and the night is cold. If I wait until daylight—"

Dark Moon made an almost threatening gesture, and instinctively Susannah shrank back. "You wait, Black Oak never let you go. Take horse and make for caves to the east. You find shelter there," she said.

"How far are these caves?" Susannah asked, but Dark Moon merely gestured once more toward the door-flap.

"Go now. Some day we meet again."

A prediction or a promise? Susannah wondered. With the bundle of her spare clothes under one arm and a blanket around her shoulders, Susannah walked toward Gray Wolf's lodge.

If he had returned, she would challenge him to deny what Dark Moon had told her about the binding ceremony. If, as she suspected, he wasn't there, she would simply seize the opportunity to take some of Gray Wolf's provisions.

She'd certainly have need of them to get back to Kentucky.

six

It was far easier than Susannah would have thought possible to escape from the village. In Gray Wolf's lodge she found his bridle and saddle and took a leather trail pouch filled with parched corn and strips of jerky.

Getting a horse from the corral had been the hardest part, especially when the animals began to whinny and mill around, causing the village dogs to bark and waking the young boy who was supposed to be guarding the horses. But by the time he had stumbled sleepily to the corral, Susannah had already slipped the bridle on the nearest horse and led it into the cover of the nearby woods. Had the boy stopped to count the animals, Susannah might never have gotten away, but apparently it never occurred to him to do such a thing. By the time the boy had gone back to sleep, she had already saddled the horse and headed south toward the Ohio River.

Knowing that she would certainly be missed in the morning and that her pursuers would likely take the same trail to search for her, Susannah chose a more easterly direction. The Hunters had spoken of a narrow place in the river where a horse and rider could usually ford, and if such a place existed, she determined to find it.

Silently thanking her father for the woodsmanship he had taught his children, Susannah rode slowly through the forest. As she came out into meadow, she noted with alarm that the moonlight, so bright earlier in the evening, had now been greatly diminished by a bank of clouds. Lifting her face to the night air, Susannah smelled snow. It wouldn't be a deep fall, but even a light dusting would leave tracks that would be plain enough for anyone to read. Susannah urged her horse to a faster gait, attempting to cover as much ground as she could before the snow began.

Susannah estimated that she had been on the trail some two hours when the first snowflakes stung her cheeks. At the next creek, Susannah dismounted and checked the depth of the water. Seeing that it was shallow, she remounted and urged her horse to pick its way through it for a distance. Then as the stream seemed to be deepening and the horse showed a marked reluctance to continue in it, Susannah returned to shore and made for some low hills that gave promise of holding the caves Dark Moon had mentioned.

Let there be some large enough to hide me, she prayed when her preliminary exploration revealed only shallow depressions.

A fresh wind began to blow, and the snow swirled ever harder as Susannah continued to search the rocky hills. Finally she came to an overhanging ledge, under which she could make out a gaping black hole. Susannah led her horse down the slight incline to the mouth of the cave and peered inside. It was impossible to see how deep the cave was, but its entrance was high enough to accommodate both her and the horse. Susannah tugged on the bridle until the animal reluctantly entered the darkness.

After a time Susannah's eyes grew accustomed enough to the gloom to make out a few boulders strewn on the cave floor. She tied the reins around a large stone, then she brushed aside enough of the small rocks littering the cave floor to make a place to lie down in relative comfort.

Susannah had noticed a rather rank odor when she first entered the cave, and as soon as she lay down and pulled up her blanket, she heard a low growl that raised the hairs on the back of her neck and made the horse whinny in fright.

Susannah tensed and waited for the sound to be repeated. *What was it?* She began to think of the wild animals that would likely hole up in a cave in the dead of winter, and stopped when she came to the most obvious one.

Bears like to sleep the winter through in a nice, warm cave, her father had told her. More than once, Jonathan McKay said, he and Nate McIntyre had shared a cave with a hibernating bear. "They won't bother you unless you disturb their rest," Nate had said when asked if it was dangerous.

I hope they're right, Susannah thought. The bear growled once more, then Susannah heard shuffling sounds as it apparently moved into a more comfortable position before settling down to sleep again.

Susannah was too tired to go anywhere else, and almost as soon as she closed her eyes, she slept.

&

From the time she was a child, Susannah had never been able to remember many of her dreams. Occasionally when she awoke she could recall a fragment or two of the images that came to her in the night, but such occasions were rare. After James had been killed, she used to lie awake night after night, hoping first that she could sleep at all, and then that she would dream of their happy days together. Even though such dreams were a poor substitute for the man she had loved for so long, they would have been some ease for the aching void in her heart. James had never had his likeness sketched, and now his easy smile, flashing green eyes, and cleft chin existed only in Susannah's memory.

If I could dream of him, it'd almost be like we were together again, Susannah thought, but night after night her wish had been denied.

Some time later, even though Susannah was awake enough to be aware of the hardness of the cave floor beneath her, she felt lips touching hers, and knew a rush of joy that at last she must be dreaming of James.

The lips that pressed tenderly on hers were surprisingly warm and so lifelike that Susannah put her hand out to touch his face, then circled both arms around his neck to draw him even closer.

How can a dream seem so real? some part of her being asked, but even as Susannah began to awaken, she tightened her hold, reluctant to let go of this brief respite from her grief.

"Sehe!" a man's voice warned, and instantly Susannah's eyes flew open.

A hand covered her mouth before she could utter the scream that died in her throat as she realized who was bending over her.

Gray Wolf. Had he really kissed her, or had that been part of her dream?

Susannah struggled to sit up, but Gray Wolf held her forearms in such a tight grip that she gasped. "Let me go! Why did you follow me?" she asked, whispering in deference to the other occupant of the cave.

"Why you run away?"

"I had to," she said, reluctant to disclose what Dark Moon had told her.

A momentary look of pain crossed Gray Wolf's face. "Black Oak is angry that his daughter does not accept his gift of her life."

"Daughter?" Susannah repeated. "Is that what that was all about last night?"

Gray Wolf loosened his grip on her arms and sat back on his heels. "Black Oak has no daughters. By binding us, you his daughter now, same as I am son. It is so for life."

"Why didn't you tell me all that last night?" she asked. "I thought—"

Gray Wolf's mouth twisted. "I know what you think, I know why you run away."

Susannah pulled herself up to a sitting position and looked at him with all the appeal her brown eyes could muster. "Then let me go back to my people."

"You go to the river, you die there," Gray Wolf said matter-of-factly.

"Then take me across—you must know the way," she pleaded. "My people will pay gold for me."

"Your people!" Gray Wolf said with contempt. "Your people pay fire and bullets. It is all they know. You better off here in this cave with bear than go back to *schwannack*."

"No one will harm you if you are with me," Susannah said. She touched her fist to her heart as she had seen Gray Wolf do. "It is so."

Gray Wolf shook his head and stood. "I know *schwannack*. It is not so."

Susannah rose to her feet and put a detaining hand on his sleeve. "You must know that you are white yourself," she said. "What makes you so angry with your own kind?"

Gray Wolf looked down at her for a long moment as if he wanted to say something but had no words to express it, then he took a step backward, shaking off her arm. "It is not your concern," he said. "There will be no more talk of this. We ride back to village now."

"What will Black Oak do to me?" Susannah asked.

"If he think you have good reason to leave, nothing," he said. "If he think you spy—"

"I had a good reason," Susannah said.

Gray Wolf's lips compressed in a grim line. "So you say," he said. "Come now. The dawn grows old. Enemies likely near."

"What enemies?" Susannah asked. "What do you mean?"

"Not all those against us are *schwannack*," he said, and from the tone of his voice Susannah knew it was unlikely that Gray Wolf would tell her more.

"The raid you just made—it wasn't against whites?"

"I have said all I will say. *Schwannack* women ask much."

A faint smile lifted the corners of Susannah's mouth. "I am

not *schwannack*. I am Su-sannah, daughter of the mighty Black Oak."

Gray Wolf did not seem amused. "He should hear you say it."

They broke their fast at the mouth of the cave and, by leaning over and letting the water splash into their mouths, they drank from a cold spring nearby. The snow had stopped in the night, and as they led their horses out of the rocks, the sun came out again.

"How did you find me?" Susannah asked. "I rode in the creek."

"Tracks go in, go out. Many tracks around cave."

"You came alone," she said. "Why?"

Gray Wolf looked exasperated. "No more talk," he said. "No—more—talk." He dug his heels in the side of his horse and rode away from her.

He is a strange man, Susannah thought as she slapped the reins against her horse's withers and followed him. The white Indian had saved her life, only to put her in jeopardy again, not once, but twice. He pretended not to feel deeply about anything, yet she sensed a great sadness in his past, and—

Susannah didn't have to close her eyes to remember how thoroughly she had been kissed as she awoke that morning. Dreams weren't flesh and blood, but mere phantoms, incapable of physical contact. What she had felt was too real to be a dream. Gray Wolf must have really kissed her.

Gray Wolf does feel deeply, Susannah realized. Perhaps one day he would even admit it to himself.

❧

About the same place where Susannah had started to smell the village campfires on the day Gray Wolf had brought her there from the river, she once again smelled smoke. But this time the odor was a great deal more acrid and accompanied by a smudge of black that hung on the horizon.

Gray Wolf turned to Susannah and pointed to the pall of smoke. "See? This is work our enemies know best."

Without another word, Gray Wolf galloped away from her. Susannah followed, a hollow feeling gathering in the pit of her stomach. She feared that something terrible had happened, and what she saw when she rode into Black Oak's village confirmed that it had come under a savage attack, probably only that very morning.

The scene was one of confusion and devastation. Several lodges had already burned to the ground, while one or two others still smoldered. A trail of dropped plunder led through the village and past the empty corral. Several dead or dying women and children lay scattered around their ruined lodges, along with a few warriors who must have tried to defend them.

Gray Wolf reached the village first and squatted over a still form in front of Black Oak's lodge. Susannah dismounted and led her horse into the center of the village, increasingly dismayed by the sights and sounds around her. Somewhere a child cried and a woman wailed as the dazed survivors began to emerge from the woods and still-standing lodges and search for theirfamilies.

Seeing that Dark Moon's lodge had not been fired, Susannah tied the horse to a sapling near it and stooped to enter. The old woman lay on the ground on the other side of the fire. Susannah started toward her and nearly tripped over the body that lay just inside the entrance.

An Indian, Susannah confirmed, but not Delaware. From his topknot and war paint, the man must have been a Shawnee. He lay on his back, with the long knife Dark Moon had used both to save and to threaten Susannah protruding from his chest.

With a shudder, Susannah stepped over him and went to Dark Moon. "Are you all right?" she asked, but the old woman did not answer. When Susannah felt for a pulse, she saw that

Dark Moon's forehead had been cut, probably in an effort to scalp her.

The cut wasn't deep, but blood from it had run into the old woman's eyebrows and face, making her injury look far worse. Susannah found a container of water and a scrap of linen and scrubbed, then bound, the jagged wound. Dark Moon groaned once, but said nothing, even when she opened her eyes and appeared to be staring directly at Susannah.

"You are not badly hurt," Susannah told her, but the old woman merely groaned and closed her eyes, either fainting or pretending to.

Susannah had tied off the crude bandage and turned to leave when she noticed that the dead Indian, who had a tomahawk in his right hand, held something else in his left. Although his hand was closed around it, a rawhide loop trailed from it. Susannah figured that the man must have struck Dark Moon a blow with his tomahawk, then taken her cross. Before he could turn to leave, Dark Moon's knife had found his chest, and the Indian had died clutching Susannah's wooden cross.

He probably had no idea what it means to those who follow Christ. Susannah felt a pang for the soul of the heathen who had tried to take Dark Moon's life.

Susannah knelt by the man and prized his fingers open, finally freeing the cross from his grasp. She hastily slipped it on over her head, hiding it beneath her deerskin shift, lest anyone take it from her again.

Susannah stepped back outside. Seeing that Black Oak stood talking with Gray Wolf, she felt a sense of relief that the village chief still lived. From the look of things, the people already had enough problems without having to deal with the death of their chief.

Susannah started toward the men, then stopped as she heard Black Oak speak her name in anger. Although she couldn't make out all of Black Oak's words, the chief seemed to be blaming Gray Wolf for making Su-sannah run away, then for going after her and leaving the village when it needed his strength to defend it.

"The woman is bound to you. You must control her," Black Oak said.

"I could easier control the wind, my father," Gray Wolf replied.

"You are not *netopalis,* then. A true warrior does these things."

Gray Wolf shifted from one foot to another and looked down at the ground. He said something too low for Susannah to hear, then he turned and looked directly at her as if he had suddenly sensed that she watched him. "Come here," he called.

Susannah approached them and bowed to Black Oak. She said nothing, nor did she look directly at nor speak to either man.

"You are one of us now," Black Oak said in tones he might have used with a backward child. "You stay with Gray Wolf. We will have no more trouble about this."

Susannah nodded again. "You have said it, *muchomes.*"

Black Oak turned back to Gray Wolf as if he hadn't heard her. "Find your brothers and tell them to prepare the people to move."

"Where do we go, Father?" Gray Wolf asked.

"To my brother's village. If they have returned, they will share what they have with us. If they are still gone, perhaps we will have shelter."

Gray Wolf struck his breast with his fist and then turned to Susannah. "You hear the words of Black Oak. Stay in my lodge until we go."

Susannah started to protest, then saw the look on Black Oak's face and thought better of it. Instead, she nodded. To both men she said, "Dark Moon still lives. A warrior cut her, but she killed him with her knife. He lies in her lodge."

"Dappled Faun will see to her needs," Black Oak said. "Now, go."

With both men watching her, Susannah had no choice but to bow to them and walk back to what was left of Gray Wolf's lodge. However, her mind was already busy.

I'll get away somehow, Susannah promised herself. She touched her hand to the comforting outline of the cross. In the hope that God could hear her, even among these strangely familiar heathens, she bowed her head and haltingly recited the Lord's Prayer. When she neared the end, she stopped short and opened her eyes.

Deliver us from evil.

In this foreign place, how was she to know what—or who— was evil?

Susannah had been brought up to believe that all men were God's creation and had immortal souls and the capacity for both good and evil. Her own experience had taught her that no one, white or Indian, was all good or all bad, but that each must be judged individually. Until recently, she'd had little trouble knowing who could be trusted. Now, however—

Susannah sighed and looked back at Dark Moon's lodge, where the enigmatic woman lay alone, near the corpse of the man she had killed. At times, the old woman seemed to be her friend, yet Susannah sensed that she could also turn on her. In fact, perhaps Dark Moon already had.

She must have told Gray Wolf to look for me in the caves.

The thought came to Susannah with almost physical force. Although the old woman had urged her to get away when she still had the chance, perhaps Dark Moon had, for some reason, changed her mind and decided she didn't really want Susannah to leave, after all.

It must have something to do with Gray Wolf, Susannah thought. It was a puzzle her mind could pick at, but never solve.

Deliberately she made herself finish the prayer. *Deliver us from evil. For thine is the kingdom, and the power, and the glory, for ever. Amen.*

Susannah sighed and touched her hand to her cross once more, but the gesture brought her no comfort.

≈

Within the hour, Gray Wolf returned to his lodge and silently gathered what little the raiding Shawnee had left of his possessions.

"Dark Moon had something of mine. I would like to look for it," Susannah said when it was clear that Gray Wolf wasn't going to speak to her.

Gray Wolf gave her an annoyed look. "I go with you," he said.

Dark Moon was sitting up when they entered her lodge, only the white bandage around her forehead indicating that anything unusual had happened. The dead Indian was gone, and most of Dark Moon's belongings had been neatly bundled. She looked up at them when they entered, but said nothing.

"What you want here?" Gray Wolf asked Susannah.

"It's probably in there," Susannah said, pointing to the bundle.

"No time to look. You carry it to corral." Without waiting for a reply, Gray Wolf left the lodge.

"How do you feel? Can you walk?" Susannah asked Dark Moon in English.

At first she thought the old woman wasn't going to answer, but as Susannah turned away to leave, Dark Moon made a low sound deep in her throat. "I walk. You walk, too," she said. "You go with us."

"For now, I must," Susannah replied. *But not for always.*

Susannah picked up the heavy bundle and left. She didn't look back at Dark Moon nor see the tears that streamed down the old woman's creased cheeks.

≈

The march to Running Beaver's village took place in an almost eerie silence. The men went first, followed by the women and children. No one had to be told not to speak, and all instantly obeyed the hand signals of the lead scouts.

Susannah carried Dark Moon's bundle. She hadn't had a chance to see if it contained her coins, but from the way the burden seemed to grow heavier with each mile, she thought it must contain many coins, along with assorted rocks. Susannah wanted to ask how far it was to Running Beaver's village, but Gray Wolf was nowhere to be seen, and the women around her paid her no heed. Dark Moon walked just in front of the children, half-supported by Dappled Faun. Susannah marveled that the old woman was able to keep up with the others as they pressed on with only rare stops to rest, no food, and only a mouthful of water as the day wore on.

Darkness will overtake us before we get there, Susannah thought as the pale winter sun slipped out of sight, replaced by a chill purple twilight. She didn't relish the thought of walking at night in unfamiliar territory, when the temperature could drop many degrees and they would be at the mercy of any number of human and animal predators.

Soon the leaders quickened their pace, and in deep twilight they topped a final hill, stopped, and gazed down into the village of their destination.

Like all Delaware villages, it was built in a meadow by a fairly large stream. Running Beaver's village was larger than the one they had left, and its steam house and most of its lodges were still intact. But no welcome smoke arose from the dwellings and no cooking fires dotted the village as they should at this hour of the evening.

"It is the same as before," a woman beside Susannah said to another. "Running Beaver's people are gone."

What will we do? Susannah wondered, unconsciously using the first person, and from behind her a soft feminine voice spoke.

"We wait here. The scouts make sure no one waits to attack us," Dappled Faun said as she walked up to join Susannah.

"How is Dark Moon?" Susannah asked.

The girl shrugged. "She is always the same," she replied, implying that Susannah had been foolish to ask.

"If you need help with her…," Susannah begin, but Dappled Faun shook her head.

"She ask if you have her bundle. I go back and tell her."

Dark Moon's mind must still be clear, Susannah thought. Perhaps she'd have a chance to learn more from her if they could once more share a lodge. But Black Oak had said she must stay with Gray Wolf.

Susannah sighed and wrapped her blanket around her shoulders, trying not to think about that.

Soon the scouts returned and conferred briefly with Black Oak. While they shivered in the growing cold, Black Oak sent one man into the village.

"Wanega goes to make sure there are no evil spirits," Susannah heard someone say.

"Wanega's medicine not strong against the Shawnee," another commented.

Susannah considered the implications of the woman's words. Perhaps the Shawnee had chased away Running Beaver and his people, or perhaps they had fled from white settlers seeking revenge for raids on their lands in Kentucky. In either case, Susannah surmised that Black Oak would not think it was safe to stay there long, with or without the approval of the Medicine Man.

"We go on now," the word finally came. Susannah stumbled down the hill in the shadowy light of the waning moon, hoping that soon she could know the comfort of a fire and hot food.

The moment that Susannah stepped onto the flat meadow upon which the village had been built, Gray Wolf appeared by her side. "Come with me," he said.

Susannah followed him to a lodge that had been stripped of

all its furnishings. No skins littered the floor or hung on the bare walls. It would furnish them some protection from the elements, but that was about all.

"Can we have a fire?" Susannah asked.

"In time," Gray Wolf said. "Open Dark Moon's bundle and prepare her bed. I will bring her here."

Relieved, Susannah began to tug on the bundle's rawhide bindings as Gray Wolf reappeared in the doorway. "Do not leave this place," he added, and disappeared again.

As if I could, Susannah thought wearily. They had walked northwest for several hours, every step taking them farther from the Ohio River and dimming Susannah's hopes of getting back to Kentucky on her own. The horse she had ridden the night before and two or three others were all that had been left after the Shawnee's raid on Black Oak's village. The horses would be closely guarded now, as would Susannah herself. There was almost no chance that she would be able to get away again. At the moment, however, Susannah was too cold and too tired to want to go anywhere.

Gray Wolf returned with an armful of firewood, Dark Moon following him. The old woman said nothing to either of them, but lay down on the skins Susannah had spread and immediately fell asleep.

After kindling a fire, Gray Wolf again left without saying anything further. Susannah bent over the flames, grateful for their warmth. She was still hungry, but so tired that she knew she'd sleep.

"Get up and eat," Gray Wolf ordered.

Susannah sat up and took the offered parched corn and jerky. "What about Dark Moon?" she asked.

Gray Wolf glanced at the old woman, whose breathing already bordered onto snoring, and shook his head. "She sleep now. She eat tomorrow."

"This is good," Susannah said. "Is there water?"

Gray Wolf handed her his leather canteen.

"Thank you," she said. When she had drunk her fill, she handed it back and he raised it to his lips.

"Now you sleep," Gray Wolf said, and obediently Susannah lay back down.

Despite Black Oak's order, Susannah half-expected Gray Wolf to leave again, but after hanging his canteen from a lodgepole, he put a few more sticks on the fire and lay down with his head at her feet. Soon his even breathing told her he slept.

Oddly comforted by his presence, Susannah closed her eyes and once more wished that she might dream of James.

But the man in Susannah's confused tangle of thoughts that might have been dreams, the man who held her hand as they rode together into some nameless, shapeless danger, then stopped to kiss her—that man wasn't James.

seven

When Susannah awoke the next morning, Dark Moon sat opposite her, feeding twigs to the fire, and Gray Wolf was gone. She seemed calm, and Susannah hoped that she might now be willing to talk of the past.

"How are you?" Susannah asked in English.

Dark Moon put her hand to the bandage on her head and shrugged. "My head hurts. I am hungry."

Susannah held out the deerhide pouch. "Here—Gray Wolf brought food."

Without comment Dark Moon ate what was left, then drank deeply from Gray Wolf's canteen.

"Gray Wolf is a good son to you," Susannah said.

Dark Moon frowned and stared at Susannah, and from the look that came over her features, Susannah feared that the old woman might be about to retreat again into madness. However, when she finally spoke, her voice was calm and matter-of-fact. "Gray Wolf is not my son."

Susannah's exclamation of surprise brought a faint smile to Dark Moon's face. "He isn't? But you're both white—"

Dark Moon interrupted, speaking forcefully. "He does not want it. Never speak to him of it."

Susannah leaned forward in her eagerness to learn more about Gray Wolf. "But why does he hate white people so much?"

Dark Moon sighed heavily and looked sad. "Fair Star," she said, then stopped as if she didn't intend to say more.

"Fair Star was Gray Wolf's wife?" Susannah guessed.

The old woman nodded, then paused to wipe tears from her eyes. "When *schwannack* killed her parents, I took her into my lodge. I gave her to Gray Wolf, then—"

Dark Moon's voice broke and she buried her face in her hands, unable to continue. But she had no need to; Susannah immediately understood what must have befallen her.

"How long ago was that?" she asked.

Dark Moon dug at her eyes with the palms of her hands and sighed heavily. "Last year just before first frost. Gray Wolf went after *schwannack,* but they got away."

Susannah put her hand on Dark Moon's. "I am sorry."

Dark Moon took Susannah's hand and turned it over, exposing the red line where it had been cut. "Gray Wolf needs a wife. You need a husband. Don't run from him again."

"You sent him after me," Susannah said accusingly. The old woman took her hand from Susannah's wrist and sat back on her haunches in silence. Softening her voice, Susannah spoke again. "I must go home. My people in Kentucky—"

"You have no man there," Dark Moon interrupted.

"Why do you say that?" Susannah asked.

Dark Moon pointed to the golden band encircling Susannah's finger. "The man who gave you this ring does not come for you."

"You do not know so. Many will follow me here," Susannah said, still reluctant to confirm Dark Moon's suspicion that she was a widow.

Susannah had spoken the truth: there were many who would willingly rescue her, if only they knew where to look. That someone else had survived the flatboat attack and returned to Lexington with the news that she was alive might be unlikely, but Susannah knew it was still possible that she was being sought.

"I once thought the same," Dark Moon said. "No one comes. You will learn."

"How did you happen to come to the Lenni-Lenape?" Susannah asked, but Dark Moon made the cut-off sign, abruptly ending the conversation.

"Enough talk," she said. "Now you must go after wood. The fire burns low."

Susannah took the rolled-up mat in which Gray Wolf had brought wood the night before, put a blanket around her shoulders, and went outside. Thick clouds covered the sun, and a mean wind tugged at the trees. Many of the women and children seemed to be resting in the lodges vacated by Running Beaver's people, and Susannah supposed that the men had gone in search of game.

No one paid Susannah any heed as she climbed the hill behind the village and entered a stand of mixed evergreens and hardwood trees. Apparently many others had been there before her and had already gathered the branches and twigs that lay on the ground within easy reach. Rather than go deeper into the woods, Susannah turned south and gathered fallen wood as she walked. She stopped beside a tangle of bushes entwined with dry vines that would kindle a fire well.

As she pulled a thick, twisted vine from a shrub it had encircled, an eerie sensation overcame Susannah and she shivered, but not from the cold.

I have been here before and I have done this very thing.

But of course she could not possibly have been here in the Indian Territory, nor should her wood-gathering task seem familiar. Even while she was growing up in Carolina and learning to do many chores that her Indian mother had learned in her own childhood, Susannah had never collected firewood— her brothers always did that.

I picked berries, though, she recalled. *And we gathered nuts each fall. That must be why this all seems so natural.*

In her mind's eye Susannah saw her mother giving them willow and oak baskets she had woven, baskets they would fill to overflowing with hazel and hickory nuts, chestnuts and walnuts. As they worked, Sukeu-quawon told her children stories of the old ways and the old days, long before her own time, when the Lenni-Lenape had lived far away to the northeast, and the white man had not yet found the other side of the big river-ocean.

"My people always used the gifts of the forest and meadow wisely. In return we had meat to eat and grain to plant. It is not so now."

When she spoke of those times, the usually cheerful and smiling Sukeu-quawon seemed to be thoughtful, almost sad. Yet when Susannah asked her mother if she ever wished she had stayed in her village on the Monongahela, her denial had been immediate and vigorous.

"God sent Jonathan McKay to be my husband. A woman belongs with her husband. This is so with white people as well as the Lenni-Lenape. So one day it will be with you, little daughter."

Susannah had been only a child when her mother had died, but her mother's influence and imprint had never completely faded, partly because Susannah's father had continued to speak of her, often and freely, even after he had married again.

Susannah still remembered her sense of betrayal when she learned that her father had married a widow with two children. She had run away from her Aunt Sarah Stone's house, where she and her brothers had lived since their mother's death, and hidden in the hay in Squire Boone's barn. Jonathan McKay had found her there and held her close. They had wept together for a time before her father wiped the tears from Susannah's eyes and assured her that he would always honor the memory of her mother.

"Had I been taken, Sukey would ha'e done the same," he told her. "God bound us as one until death parted us, but He dinna mean for us to spend the rest of our lives grieving. 'Tis a sin for a Christian to worship the dead."

Susannah hadn't understood all of what her father had told

her that day—even now, after she had buried a husband she
had adored, it was hard for Susannah to accept that her life
had gone on without him.

*Oh, James, why did we ever leave Carolina? And why didn't
I wait for my father to come for me, instead of trying to set out
on my own?*

Susannah's eyes stung with tears, but deliberately she blinked
them back. What had happened in the past was done with, and
all the tears of a lifetime would never change one heartbeat
that had gone before. What happened to her from now on,
however, was a different matter. Every choice she had made
since James's murder had produced its own consequences, and
she knew that other choices awaited her.

How can I know what I should do? Susannah cried silently.

As if her mother stood beside her, Susannah could almost
hear the solution Sukeu-quawon had proposed for every prob-
lem. *Pray about it, my daughter.*

Yes, but how?

Susannah folded the mat with the twigs and vines and tucked
it under her left arm, freeing her hand to reach inside her shift
for her mother's cross. Holding it tightly, Susannah closed her
eyes and prayed aloud.

"Lord, I need help and guidance and I don't know what to
do. Show me the path I should follow and lead me in it. Amen."

Susannah stood for a moment, alert to hear anything different in the sounds of the forest around her, but only the whining
of the wind answered her. Oddly disappointed that nothing
seemed to have changed, she reached for the next likely source
of wood, a dead branch lodged in a tree just over her head.

What did you expect? Susannah chided herself for halfway
expecting an immediate answer. No bush would burst into flame
to prove that God had a message for her. *Almighty God is not
to be ordered about like a servant,* Adam Craighead had
preached. *Man's whim may not be God's will.*

Almost angrily Susannah tugged at the branch with one hand. When it didn't yield to her efforts, she dropped her mat bundle and used both hands to dislodge it. The branch loosened, struck a glancing blow to her head, and scratched the side of her face as it fell.

"Ouch!" Susannah exclaimed. She put a hand to her stinging cheek and felt a trickle of blood. The cut didn't seem to be deep, but it would need to be cleansed.

Susannah bent and picked up the mat, then with the other hand she grasped the heavy end of the fallen limb. Dragging it behind her, she retraced her steps. With her naturally good sense of direction and the woodcraft skills her parents had taught her, Susannah had no trouble threading her way past trees that all looked the same and emerging from the woods at almost the exact point at which she had entered.

Susannah stopped at the top of the hill to get a better grip on the mat bundle and saw Gray Wolf and Black Oak emerge from the chief's lodge. They stood, apparently engaged in earnest conversation. From their gestures, Susannah thought they might be arguing, but after seeming to make a threatening gesture, Black Oak reached out and touched Gray Wolf's shoulder. Gray Wolf inclined his head, then brought his fist to his chest and turned away. Neither man glanced toward the place where she stood silhouetted against the darkening sky, nor did Susannah try to attract their attention.

Perhaps Gray Wolf will come seeking me, Susannah thought. For some reason, the thought was not unpleasant.

Despite the cold and her slight injuries, Susannah's heart lifted as she started down the steep hill. She glanced at Gray Wolf, who seemed to be going toward the lodge where they had all slept the previous night. Susannah had gotten about halfway down the hill when her foot slipped on loose pebbles. She cried out, dropped the wood she carried, and vainly fought to keep her balance. Susannah fell heavily to the ground and tumbled and rolled for what seemed to be an eternity before her body finally came to rest only inches from a large rock.

❧

Although Gray Wolf knew it would probably be futile, he had made one last appeal to Black Oak to allow him to go alone to see Okega-Muga. The chief would not hear his request, cutting him off as soon as he began to speak.

"The woman Su-sannah may be near kin to Okega-Muga. He will be obliged to help us if she asks it."

"If this is not so, Okega-Muga will be angry with you for sending her. It is better for the woman to stay here."

Black Oak's voice held a dangerous edge of anger. "Why do you make trouble with this? You know the woman must be watched if she stays here."

"Dark Moon will keep her close by her side. There will be no trouble if she stays."

Black Oak scowled and made the cut-off sign. "You know better than this. I will hear no more of it."

Gray Wolf touched his fist to his heart. "As you say, Father."

"One thing more—"

Gray Wolf turned back to Black Oak and waited.

"Watch how you treat Su-sannah. Running Fox watches you both."

Gray Wolf's lips tightened, but he nodded again and said nothing. The friction that had always existed between him and his brother had grown greater each time Running Fox imagined he had been slighted in favor of Gray Wolf. However, Black Oak had always been careful to treat his sons alike—that was not Running Fox's complaint.

Gray Wolf started to the lodge where he had left Susannah and thought of the cause of the trouble between him and Running Fox. It had started when Dark Moon chose the younger Gray Wolf to marry her ward, Fair Star. Even now, more than a year after Fair Star's death, Running Fox had neither forgotten nor forgiven what he had taken as an insult.

Gray Wolf sighed as he recalled his reaction the night that Dark Moon had come to tell him that Fair Star would live in his lodge.

"Running Fox is older. He should take a wife first," Gray Wolf had told her, but the old woman merely laughed her crazy laugh and told him that Black Oak had already ordered the binding ceremony.

"I must give her to you because it is her wish," Dark Moon had added.

Gray Wolf had been obligated to take to wife the quiet maiden who seldom spoke, but who bore a great burden of sadness that not even Gray Wolf had been able to make her forget. He had accepted and then returned her love, and Fair Star had trusted him to care for her. Yet in the time of her greatest need, he had been too far away to help her.

But those things belong in the past, Gray Wolf told himself. Following the Delaware custom, no one had spoken her name for a year. However, the period of mourning had already been over for several months. Now Gray Wolf had been bound to another, and the chief had ordered that he must travel a long way with her.

Su-sannah will not like it, Gray Wolf thought. He had asked to make the journey alone, not because he didn't find Su-sannah attractive, but because he did. He had tried without success to forget the irresistible softness of her lips that had beckoned him to kiss her as she had slept in the bear's cave. Nor could he forget the way her arms had twined around his neck as she had pulled him closer and kissed him back.

She was asleep. She didn't know what she was doing, Gray Wolf had told himself the many times he relived those few moments. She had a man among the whites, and any day now he might come to ransom her.

In any case, Black Oak had bound them, and like it or not,

until someone else with a better claim relieved him of her, Gray Wolf had to take care of Su-sannah. The sooner the woman realized that she had the same responsibility toward him, the better it would be for them both. He must manage her or risk losing her to Running Fox.

She certainly wouldn't like him any better, Gray Wolf thought as he entered the lodge. A commotion sounded outside, and he turned to look back. Just before his view was blocked by curious villagers, Gray Wolf saw a crumpled form lying on the ground, recognized that it was Su-sannah, and immediately ran toward her.

The noise also reached into Black Oak's lodge, and fearing that the village might be under attack again, the chief picked up his tomahawk and joined the others who had already emerged from the lodges to see what was happening.

"It is Gray Wolf's woman," someone said, and the crowd parted to let Black Oak through.

Without registering either surprise or dismay that his newly-acquired daughter lay in an untidy heap at the bottom of the hill, Black Oak extended his hand to help Susannah to her feet.

Immediately Gray Wolf joined them, his face a study of mixed emotions.

Black Oak turned to him and frowned his displeasure. "What does this woman do here?"

"I do not know," Gray Wolf said. "I left her in my lodge."

Susannah pointed up the hill, where the material she had gathered was strewn where it had landed when she began her fall. "I went for wood. The fire was almost dead," she said.

"Go to the lodge," Gray Wolf said in a low voice.

Too late, Susannah realized that her words might be taken as a rebuke to Gray Wolf for not properly caring for her and Dark Moon. Even to appear to admonish a warrior in front of his chief was extremely rude, and Susannah heard the sharp intake of breath from those near enough to hear the exchange.

"Wait!" Black Oak ordered Susannah. He turned to Gray Wolf. "Her head bleeds. I will call Wanega."

Gray Wolf shook his head. "The old woman can tend her. Send him instead after the wood she scattered over the hill."

The moment of lightness Susannah had experienced earlier now seemed foolish as she entered the lodge, Gray Wolf on her heels. His anger was almost palpable as he spoke sharply to Dark Moon.

"Leave us, old woman," he ordered.

Without speaking or looking directly at either of them, Dark Moon slowly rose and left the lodge. Gray Wolf faced Susannah and extended his hand toward her. Instinctively she shrank back as if she expected to be struck.

However, Gray Wolf's touch was light as his fingers brushed the knot on her forehead caused by the falling branch. "Your man beats you," he said, his tone making it a question.

"No," Susannah said quickly. "He would not do such a thing."

"You say it," Gray Wolf replied, his tone revealing that he didn't believe her.

All the white people you know must be horrible, Susannah wanted to say, but it was clear that Gray Wolf wasn't likely to want to hear her defend *schwannack* at that moment. "It is so," she said instead.

Gray Wolf frowned as his finger traced the scratch on Susannah's cheek.

"This cut must be washed," he said. "Stay here—I bring water."

Gray Wolf picked up his leather canteen and left. Susannah sat down, pulled her blanket close around her shoulders, and wished she could take back the last few minutes. If she hadn't been so intent on watching Gray Wolf, she would have paid more attention to where she was going and wouldn't have fallen and the tense scene between Black Oak and Gray Wolf wouldn't have occurred.

No wonder Gray Wolf is angry, Susannah thought. Black Oak had made it clear that Gray Wolf had failed in his task of keeping her out of trouble, thus shaming him before the whole village.

Maybe Black Oak wants to keep me alive just long enough to get a ransom from my people, she thought. Or perhaps the chief had other plans that Gray Wolf hadn't shared with her.

"Here." Gray Wolf's return interrupted her idle speculation. Susannah winced as the cold water stung her face, but she sat quietly as he cleaned the cut, then blotted it dry with a handful of moss he had brought from the spring.

"You told Black Oak that the old woman would do this," Susannah said when Gray Wolf finished and used the moss to rekindle the fire.

"Sometimes Dark Moon heals. Sometimes she also hurts," Gray Wolf said.

Thinking of the way the old woman had wielded the knife she had eventually used to kill the Shawnee, Susannah nodded. "Where is Dark Moon now?"

"In the lodge of Dappled Faun."

Susannah spread her hands in a gesture of apology. "I do not mean to make trouble," she said earnestly.

Gray Wolf sat down opposite her. His blue eyes appraised her as if he tested the truth of her words, and she looked steadily back at him. "Dark Moon say she send you into woods," he said after a moment.

"You tell Black Oak this," Susannah said.

Gray Wolf shook his head. "No. It does not matter. Tomorrow you leave this place."

Caught off-guard, Susannah wondered if she could have heard him correctly. *Maybe he is going to let me go back to Kentucky,* she thought. "Where do I go?" she asked.

"To the village of Okega-Muga."

Susannah's initial surge of hope was quickly replaced by apprehension. She had heard both her father and Nate McIntyre speak of meeting Okega-Muga years earlier, when the French and the British still fought for control of the Western frontier. Her mother had said that their septs had been closely related.

"He is a mighty chief of the Delaware," she said aloud. "Why would Black Oak send me to him?"

Gray Wolf looked at the ground. "If Okega-Muga not help us, our people soon starve."

"Is it that bad?" Susannah asked. "The warriors bring in game, and there is corn—"

"Only a little corn for now. Seed corn is gone, buried in another village. Maybe it is there still, maybe not. *Shawonese* take our food, trade goods, leave us nothing."

"The Shawnees took from you what you took from us." Susannah spoke without thinking, and immediately a hard, closed look came over Gray Wolf's face, and he stood and glared down at her.

"Running Fox is right. You look Indian but are *schwannack*. Black Oak does a hard thing to send you with me to Okega-Muga."

For the first time, Susannah realized why Gray Wolf seemed so upset that Black Oak would send her to another chief. "Who else goes?" she asked.

"No one. Black Oak wants it so. I make ready now."

Susannah wanted to ask Gray Wolf more, but as he strode from the lodge, she knew it would do no good to call after him. There was a core of stubbornness in this white Indian. Her mother had possessed the same trait, and Susannah acknowledged that she herself could sometimes be a bit stubborn.

In some ways, I'm more Indian than Gray Wolf, she thought. By their blood, it was so. By their respective upbringings, it was not. *But Gray Wolf will find out that I can be determined, too. I will get back to Kentucky, one way or another.*

A quiet voice called her name from the doorway, and Susannah turned to see Dappled Faun.

"Come in," Susannah invited in Delaware, but the girl stayed where she was and shook her head.

"Dark Moon send you this." Dappled Faun handed over a lumpy bundle wrapped in a scrap of dirty linen which Susannah instantly recognized as her missing gold coins.

"Tell her I thank her much," Susannah replied.

Dappled Faun nodded. "Dark Moon say Gray Wolf take good care of you."

Oddly touched, Susannah put her hand on the girl's. "I hope it is so," she said.

As soon as Dappled Faun left, Susannah tied the pouch with the coins around her waist. *Now I have everything that matters to me,* she thought—the coins that could save her life, the ring that symbolized her life with James, and the cross that made her feel closer to the Power that she looked to for direction.

Only a few hours before, Susannah had prayed to be shown the path she should follow. Perhaps, she reasoned, God intended to use Gray Wolf to restore her to her people, whether or not Gray Wolf still believed that God existed.

Susannah now prayed that what lay between them because they had been bound in the Indian way could be used to bring Gray Wolf back to God, while at the same time giving her a way to return to Kentucky.

Reminded of the Bible story about how the Egyptians had gladly given up their gold and goods to get rid of their Hebrew slaves after God sent plagues on the land, Susannah almost smiled.

Gray Wolf will probably be glad to see me leave, she thought. But first, she would go with him to Okega-muga.

eight

"It is time to go."

Susannah awoke and opened her eyes, but the lodge was so dark that she could scarcely make out Gray Wolf's form bending over her.

"It is still night," she said sleepily.

"Not for long."

Susannah struggled to her feet and stretched. Since leaving Kentucky, she had grown accustomed to sleeping whenever and wherever she had the chance, but she still thought longingly of the soft, warm feather ticks she had given to Nate and Hannah McIntyre.

"I want to say good-bye to Dark Moon," she said.

"The old woman sleeps," Gray Wolf said. "She knows we go."

Susannah knew that Gray Wolf must have visited Dark Moon the night before, and she wondered what he had told the old woman about their journey. *I suppose everyone in the village knows we are going on this trip alone,* Susannah thought as she left the lodge. She almost gasped as cold air filled her lungs. "It's cold," she said.

Gray Wolf handed her a shaggy cloak made from buffalo skin. "Put this on."

"Thank you—this is better," Susannah said.

"Sehe," Gray Wolf warned. Although he had been speaking English with her, he occasionally lapsed into Delaware, and Susannah realized that, even though he had learned English first, Delaware was now his main language.

With a sense of relief Susannah saw two saddled horses awaiting them, tied to a tree at the edge of the village. At their approach, the animals stamped their feet and whinnied, their breath steaming in the uncertain pre-dawn light. Knowing how few horses Black Oak's people had left, Susannah had feared that she and Gray Wolf might have to walk to Okega-Muga's village. She would not want to go afoot very far in this kind of cold weather.

Silently Gray Wolf motioned for Susannah to take the horse she had ridden in her vain escape attempt. She pulled herself into the saddle as Gray Wolf mounted the almost-white horse he had ridden in his successful pursuit of her. *How long ago that night now seems,* Susannah thought. Had he not found her, she might be safely back in Kentucky by now.

Susannah cast a final glance at the lodge where Dark Moon slept with Dappled Faun and her family, and Gray Wolf looked toward Black Oak's lodge as if he half-expected the chief to see them off. But no one appeared from the doorways of any of the lodges as they left Running Beaver's village behind.

An eerie white mist rose from the ground and obscured the horses' hoofs, and they rode in a dim, hazy world of uniform gray. Gradually what had been mere shadows emerged as shapes, then as distinct forms—a tree here, a shrub there. Finally, a pale sun struggled over the rim of the surrounding hills and brought full light to the landscape.

Susannah was disappointed to see that they traveled northwest, away from the direction in which lay the Ohio River and, just beyond it, Kentucky. After riding in silence for some time, she spoke. "How far do we go?"

"Two days' ride," Gray Wolf said.

Susannah raised her head and surveyed the sky. "The wind freshens from the west," she said. "There could be snow."

"Your man teach you that?" Gray Wolf asked.

James had no knack for predicting the weather, but Gray Wolf didn't need to know it. "My mother and father both knew the signs."

"Snow or not, we go."

A few minutes later they left a well-used path that ran close by a river and headed their horses into the underbrush.

"Where does that trail go?" Susannah asked.

"To *Shawonese* villages. *Schwannack* burned them," Gray Wolf said. "It is not good to go there now."

I wonder if Nate McIntyre had a hand in that, Susannah thought. She wished she could see, even for a moment, where they were. Some places were better to get across the Ohio River than others, but if she could make it to a trading post, she was sure someone there would help her to get back to the Kentucky side.

"We stop now," Gray Wolf said when they had been riding for several hours. After tying the horses loosely enough to allow them to forage in the dead meadow grass, he removed food from his saddlebag and motioned toward a flat rock outcropping beside the stream that bisected the meadow.

Susannah slid from the saddle and stood gingerly, stamping her feet and swinging her arms to restore her circulation.

"You not ride much," Gray Wolf observed as she joined him.

"I can keep up," Susannah replied, nettled by the implied criticism.

Gray Wolf nodded as if she had correctly answered an important question. "Eat now."

Susannah hadn't realized how hungry she was until she took the first bite. Dried fish had never been one of her favorite foods, but she ate the whole striped bass and all the parched corn that Gray Wolf had brought, then washed it down with fresh water from the stream.

"That was good," she said with a cautious smile.

Gray Wolf turned away, looking almost angry. "It is all until tonight. We go on now."

As the sun climbed higher in the sky, the temperature became quite comfortable. However, late in the afternoon, clouds covered the sun and the wind began to blow harder. Although Susannah wrapped her blanket around her and lowered her head, there was no escaping the cold that crept into the core of her being.

I was right about the turn in the weather, she told herself, but the knowledge did nothing to make her feel warmer.

"We go this way now," Gray Wolf called to her over the whine of the wind.

Gray Wolf turned so that they rode at a right angle to the wind. It was still cold, but at least the wind no longer blew in her face, where it had stung her eyes and made her nose run.

"How much farther do we go today?" Susannah asked a few minutes later, when pellets of ice began to sting her hands and cheeks.

At first she thought Gray Wolf hadn't heard. Abruptly, he rode away to the top of a nearby hill, sat looking out for a moment, and then returned.

He peered at Susannah as if judging her strength, but he did not, as James would have done, ask her if she were able to continue to ride.

"We stop soon," he said.

"I hope so," Susannah muttered.

With every mile they covered, Susannah feared that she was leaving behind any hope of getting back to Kentucky until spring brought more temperate weather. Her father and Nate McIntyre had trapped and hunted in winters like this, or worse, for years, but they were used to it, and they never traveled when storms threatened. They knew how to make cozy shelters and had the good sense to stay in them. They would never be caught in a sleet storm like this if they could help it.

I wish they were with me now, Susannah thought. Both Nate and her father would know exactly how to get back to Kentucky, and they'd waste no time in doing it, either. On the other hand, Gray Wolf seemed determined to take her just as far in the other direction as he could. Either he didn't know any better, or he was deliberately trying to kill them both.

Susannah's dark thoughts were interrupted when she realized that Gray Wolf had at last stopped and was pointing to a cabin not a hundred yards away.

"We stay here."

Susannah needed no urging to leave the saddle, but when her moccasined feet met the ice-slick ground, they slid out from under her, and she sat down with a jolt.

Gray Wolf glanced at her and Susannah thought she saw a fleeting smile. The expression soon passed, however, and he took her horse's reins and rode over to the lean-to behind the cabin, where the animals would be protected from the wind.

Susannah gained her feet with difficulty and cautiously walked to the cabin. The door opened to her touch, revealing a bare room that had obviously not been recently occupied.

"This an old trapper's cabin," Gray Wolf explained as he entered.

Susannah spread her blanket on the rough puncheon floor and briefly wondered if her father might ever have used this cabin. However, she doubted if he and Nate had ever ventured so far north into Indian Territory.

Gray Wolf picked up his rifle and started to the door. "I come back soon," he said.

"I can go after wood," she offered, but he shook his head violently.

"No! You only fall down. Stay here."

From the doorway Susannah watched Gray Wolf walk into the nearby woods, his sure feet only occasionally sliding on the icy ground.

He walks like an Indian, she thought. In fact, everything about Gray Wolf seemed to be so thoroughly Indian that his blue eyes and light hair were an almost continual surprise.

Yet, deny it as he might, Gray Wolf's heritage was all white. *I wonder if he remembers his parents,* she thought, and felt a foolish pang of sorrow that somewhere he might have relatives who were unaware that he still lived.

He does not want to be white, Dark Moon had said, and although Susannah knew the old woman's assessment was probably correct, she still wondered what had happened to his family.

Soon Susannah heard the sharp retort of a rifle, and Gray Wolf returned in a few minutes with a brace of squirrels, which he tossed at Susannah's feet.

He handed her his hunting knife. "Dress these," he ordered. "I get wood now." Without looking at Susannah to see her reaction, Gray Wolf leaned his rifle in a corner and picked up his tomahawk.

Susannah eyed the squirrels warily. "Maybe I don't know how," she said.

Gray Wolf turned and regarded her with surprise. "All Delaware women know this," he said.

"But I am not Delaware," she reminded him.

Gray Wolf hesitated for a moment, then shrugged. "*Schwannack* women know it, too. Take care—my knife is sharp."

Seeing that Gray Wolf had no intention of dressing the game for her, Susannah tucked the knife under her arm and held the limp squirrels by their tails as she went back outside. Finding a tree stump beside the cabin that would make an acceptable table, Susannah put them down and started to work. It had been some months since Susannah had skinned and gutted small game, but even though it had never been her favorite chore, she hadn't forgotten how to do it.

As she wielded Gray Wolf's knife, Susannah found herself thinking of Fair Star. She wondered what she had looked like, and imagined her preparing game for Gray Wolf. On this long trip together, surely Gray Wolf would eventually be willing to talk about his past.

If I keep asking him long enough, sooner or later he'll have to answer me.

Susannah finished her task and looked around for some place to put the residue. Ordinarily, the squirrels' entrails would be fed to the dogs, but lacking that or any way to bury the remains, Susannah decided to dispose of them in the woods. She walked a few hundred feet into the underbrush to the right of the cabin and hurled them as far as she could. To clean her hands and the blade of the knife, she brushed aside the damp top layer and wiped them on the dry leaf-fall underneath. Susannah stayed there a moment, blowing on her nearly-numb fingers and rubbing her cold hands briskly in an attempt to warm them.

A fire will surely feel good, she thought.

"Su-sannah! Where are you?"

It was the first time she had ever detected anything even remotely like alarm in Gray Wolf's voice, and Susannah feared that something had happened to him. He might have cut himself using the tomahawk to split wood, or perhaps he had spotted hostile Indians—maybe even the dreaded *schwannack.*

"I'm coming," she called back, but it took her a few moments to emerge, still slipping and sliding on the ice, from the forest.

With relief she noted that Gray Wolf seemed to be all right. He was certainly well enough to glare at her when, out of breath, she waved the knife at him in greeting.

"You not stay here," he said accusingly.

Susannah strode toward him, ready to defend her absence, but just as she got close, she felt her feet giving way beneath her and she began to slide down.

This time Gray Wolf reached out and caught her, then continued to grip her upper arms tightly. For a heartbeat they stared into each other's eyes, then Gray Wolf bit his lower lip and released her. "Go inside," he said.

Trembling from the intensity of their encounter, Susannah picked up the squirrel carcasses and went into the cabin. A load of wood lay in the floor where Gray Wolf had dumped it when he'd discovered she wasn't there, and mechanically Susannah started taking it to the fireplace. She had knelt to put in the first stick when Gray Wolf appeared beside her.

"I do this," he said, taking the wood from her arms.

Susannah turned and looked into Gray Wolf's eyes. Never had they seemed more blue, and never had they regarded her as they now did.

"I will help," she whispered.

Already off-balance from turning from the fire, Susannah felt herself swaying toward Gray Wolf at the same moment that he moved toward her. His arms circled her shoulders and he closed his eyes as he bent to place his lips on hers.

Susannah uttered a muffled exclamation, but she made no effort to escape his embrace. As if her arms moved on their own, they went around Gray Wolf's neck, and willingly her lips returned the pressure of his. When he at last took his lips from hers, Susannah pillowed her head on his shoulder and drew a long, wavering breath.

With a choked cry, Gray Wolf abruptly thrust her away. Surprised, Susannah found herself staring into eyes made icy by his sudden anger.

"What is wrong?" Susannah put her hand on Gray Wolf's arm, but he wrenched away from her and began throwing the rest of the wood into the fireplace as if each stick represented some personal demon.

Then he seized her left hand and twisted the golden band around her finger. "Is it *schwannack* way to forget your man?"

Although Gray Wolf hadn't hurt Susannah physically, his words cut her to the heart. Susannah covered her face with her hands. Her body shook with the force of the wracking sobs that seemed to fill her whole being.

I loved James with all my heart, but there is something about this man that calls out to me. How can I ever explain it to him, since I don't understand it myself?

Almost instinctively Gray Wolf held out his arms to Susannah, but at the last moment he drew back and stopped short of actually embracing her. Part of him wanted to hold and comfort her, but his hatred for anything white was stronger.

This woman still belongs to the white man whose ring she wears. Black Oak was wrong to bind us. Nothing good can come of it.

"I make fire now," Gray Wolf said.

"I would like to talk," Susannah said when she had regained her composure.

Gray Wolf busied himself with the fire and avoided looking at her. "No more talk," he said.

"But I want you to know about James—" she began.

Gray Wolf stood and glared down at her. "We see Okega-Muga tomorrow. That is only talk that matters."

Susannah wrapped her blanket closer around her and pulled her knees to rest her chin on them. "All right," she said. "But after that we talk."

Although Gray Wolf made no response, Susannah took his silence as agreement and felt that she had won a small victory.

When a few minutes later he asked her to hold the rifle while he spitted the squirrels on its barrel, Gray Wolf's voice held no anger, and he had resumed his customary impassive expression. In silence they sat together in front of the fire, each lost in thoughts that would have surprised the other.

"We sleep now," Gray Wolf said when they had finished eating.

He spread her blanket before the fire, then went to the front of the cabin, where he lay down with his feet braced against the door.

"Good night," Susannah said.

"No more talk," Gray Wolf replied, but Susannah noted that he didn't sound nearly as stern as he probably intended.

With a faint smile, Susannah rolled up in her blanket and, although it had not been a habit with her lately, she began to pray silently. *Thank you for bringing us safely this far. Help me say the right thing to Okega-Muga tomorrow.*

Susannah wanted to add something about Gray Wolf, but she hardly knew what to ask for. *Whatever happens between us, may it be Your will. Amen,* she finished.

But from her past experience, Susannah knew that recognizing God's will wouldn't necessarily be easy.

≈

As he usually did, Gray Wolf awoke just before dawn, alert and ready for whatever the day might bring. Quietly he moved across the cabin and looked down on Susannah as she slept. *She is a beautiful woman,* Gray Wolf thought. With her eyes closed, her sooty eyelashes rested on the smooth skin of her high cheekbones. He longed to kiss her awake as he had in the cave, and to feel her arms tighten around him as she had done then, and just last evening.

Can it be that this woman feels anything for me? he wondered. The morning in the cave, Su-sannah had kissed him in her sleep. But yesterday was different. She had known who he was, and far from pulling away from him, she had returned his kiss with as much feeling as it had been given.

Yet, this woman had left him once and he had no doubt she would do so again if she thought she could get back to Kentucky—and her man.

His mouth tightened and he reached a hand out to shake her shoulder.

"Su-sannah."

Reluctantly Susannah struggled awake, trying to hold on to what had been a quiet and peaceful rest, the best she had known for weeks. Even before she opened her eyes to see Gray Wolf kneeling beside her, Susannah felt his nearness. She well remembered how Gray Wolf had awakened her that morning in the bear's cave. She opened her eyes, then closed them again and waited, almost inviting Gray Wolf to kiss her as he had then.

He bent his head toward hers, then stopped suddenly. *She belongs to a white man. She will go back to him, and I will be alone again.*

"Wake up," Gray Wolf said roughly. Immediately he rose and turned away to busy himself with packing his gear.

Susannah opened her eyes and sat up, somewhat ashamed that she had behaved as if she not only expected Gray Wolf to kiss her but had hoped that he would. "I am awake," she said somewhat tartly.

"I get the horses," Gray Wolf said.

Susannah folded and rolled her sleeping blanket and put on her heavy moccasins, then she wound rawhide leggings around them, smoothed her braids, and put on the heavy riding cloak Gray Wolf had given her.

Once more they mounted their horses in the cold pre-dawn light. The ground had been whitened by a heavy frost, but the sleet storm of the day before had moved on, and soon the horizon of the eastern sky turned several shades of pink to red, boding fair weather.

As he had done the day before, Gray Wolf halted after a few hours and shared with Susannah the remainder of the food he had brought along.

"We eat at Okega-Muga's village tonight," Gray Wolf said.

"What if Okega-Muga does not welcome us?" Susannah asked.

Gray Wolf frowned. "Why do you speak of this? We are not

yet there."

"'Sufficient unto the day is the evil thereof,'" Susannah quoted, and Gray Wolf regarded her curiously.

"I do not know these words," he said.

"They're from the Bible," Susannah said. "It means people should not worry about things before they happen."

Gray Wolf frowned as if trying to recall something just out of reach.

"My mother had a Bible," he said. "She said words from it every day."

"What happened to her?" Susannah asked gently.

Gray Wolf shook his head and stood. "*Schwannack* killed her. I will not talk more of it."

White men? Susannah stared after Gray Wolf as he obliterated all traces of the small fire that had warmed them as they ate. *If white men killed his parents as well as his wife, it's no wonder that he hates them all.*

Gray Wolf sat astride his horse, a tall, proud white Indian who pretended to feel nothing and to need no one, and who now would not look directly at her.

He needs God, Susannah thought. *And Dark Moon was right—he also needs a wife.*

If she could ever get him to really talk to her, Susannah thought she might be able to help him realize his need for God. As for the other...

Susannah rode after Gray Wolf, who had started out without waiting to see if she followed.

God can take care of that, too, she knew. But Susannah wasn't quite ready to pray for Gray Wolf to find a wife. First, she needed to persuade him to help her get back to Kentucky.

nine

Susannah and Gray Wolf reached Okega-Muga's village well
before dark. The settlement was obviously older and larger than
either Black Oak's or Running Beaver's villages. The welcome
smoke from many fires hung over it like a warm blanket as
they dismounted to lead their horses into the village.

One hut stood by itself at the edge of a small stream, of a
different size and shape from the other buildings. From its
roof and the several gaps in its walls, steam mingled with the
smoke from the fires within. Susannah stopped and pointed to
it.

"I have not seen a steam house in many years," she said.

Gray Wolf looked surprised. "Dark Moon not take you to
steam house in Black Oak's village?"

"No. I didn't see one at Running Beaver's village, either."

"All Lenni-Lenape have steam house. We not at the village
of Running Beaver long enough to use it. What do you know
about this?"

Susannah was silent for a moment, remembering. "My father built my mother a steam house by the creek behind our
house. They heated big rocks in a fire and poured water over
them to make steam. I liked that part in the winter. I did not
like jumping into the cold creek afterwards."

"You still use steam house?" Gray Wolf asked.

Susannah shook her head and resumed walking toward the
main part of the village. "Oh, no—that was many years ago,
before my mother died. My stepmother didn't like the steam
house, so we quit using it."

"What is step-mother?" Gray Wolf asked, and once again

Susannah had to remind herself that, no matter how white Gray Wolf looked, there were many things he did not understand about the people of his birth.

"It is the name for the woman who married my father after my mother died."

"There is much English I do not know," Gray Wolf said.

"You speak English much better than I do Delaware," she said.

"You must not talk English with Okega-Muga," Gray Wolf said.

"What am I say to him?"

"Nothing until I tell you. Then you say you are from Clan of the Serpent. I will do other talking." Gray Wolf pointed to Susannah's cross, which she had worn openly since leaving Running Beaver's village. "Do not show that here."

"I am not ashamed to follow Christ," Susannah said. "It may be that some among Okega-Muga's people are also Christians, perhaps even the chief himself."

Gray Wolf shook his head. "I know this is not so. Black Oak and Okega-Muga once meet in council with Netawatwees. They warned him not to leave the ways of his fathers. But he did not listen. He took the name of Ab-raham and all his people followed Christ."

Susannah recalled that had been the name of the chief who, with two hundred and fifty of his followers, had met death at the hands of whites, setting off the wave of retaliatory strikes in which James and many other white settlers had died.

Susannah closed her hand around the cross. "That was a terrible thing done by *schwannack.* I will keep this around my neck, but underneath so no one sees it, if that is what you want."

"It must be done," Gray Wolf said, and Susannah had the feeling that if she had protested, he might have taken the cross from her. "The gold, also."

At first Susannah thought with a shock that Gray Wolf must knew about the coins hidden beneath her deerskin dress, then she saw that he pointed at her hand and realized that he referred to her wedding band. Silently Susannah twisted it from her finger, then unknotted the strip of rawhide holding the cross and threaded the ring through it before retying it.

"I do this to make you safe," he added in a softer tone, and Susannah realized that in his own way, whether he realized it or not, Gray Wolf was telling her that he cared for her welfare.

"I would keep us both safe," she replied.

"Then do as I say," he said.

As they entered the village, a group of curious children followed them, silently and at a safe distance.

"Which is the lodge of Okega-Muga?" Gray Wolf asked them, and as Susannah had expected, one of the older children pointed out the largest lodge in the village.

Once more, as they passed lodges and cooking fires and met the women's curious, but not unfriendly, stares, Susannah had the strange feeling that she had been in this place before, that somehow she knew these people.

They do not look at us as if we are strangers, she thought. She hoped that was a sign that the chief would welcome them.

As they neared the chief's lodge, Gray Wolf stopped to give Susannah her final instructions. "You come inside with me now, but when Okega-Muga offers the pipe, you go stay with women. You not talk unless I say."

"I know," Susannah replied. She had heard her mother speak of the rituals of greeting that must take place before any real business could be transacted. The process of asking Okega-Muga for help might take some time, but it must not be rushed.

Near the chief's lodge, a caldron of stew hung suspended from a tripod of sticks over a cooking fire, sending a pleasing aroma into the crisp air. As Susannah inhaled the tantalizing fumes, her stomach rumbled loudly.

From Gray Wolf's expression, she knew he must have heard it. "We eat later," he said.

"You and the chief must talk fast," Susannah said, and once

more she thought she detected a faint smile before Gray Wolf looked away.

A warrior emerged from the chief's lodge and nodded to a young boy to take their horses. He folded his arms across his chest and stared at Gray Wolf.

"Auween kachev?"

"I am Gray Wolf, son of Okega-Muga's friend Black Oak."

"Black Oak?" the young man repeated. "And the woman?"

"She is called Su-sannah," Gray Wolf replied. "We come in peace to speak to your mighty chief."

"I am Exundas, the son of Okega-Muga. I do not know if my father will see you."

Susannah smiled at the young man. "Please tell Okega-Muga that we have come a long way to visit the mighty chief."

Gray Wolf shot a quick looked at Susannah and frowned.

"I will ask my father," he said, and left them.

"No more talk," Gray Wolf warned. "Stand behind me. I tell you if I want you to talk."

Before Susannah had the chance to point out that Black Oak must have had a reason for sending her along, Exundas returned and motioned for them to enter.

Although Okea-Muga's lodge was much larger than either Black Oak's or Running Beaver's, it did not have nearly as many skins on the walls and floor. The young warrior who had first spoken to them stood to the right beside the chief, and a young girl of perhaps eleven or twelve sat on the other side. Behind, ranged in the traditional half circle, sat a half-dozen council members.

Susannah had expected the legendary Okega-Muga to be hearty and robust and large in stature. She was surprised to see a small man, frail and bowed with the weight of his years. His robe of buffalo skins all but obscured his lined face, but a keen intelligence shone from his eyes as he warily watched Susannah and Gray Wolf approach.

Gray Wolf bowed deeply before the old man and spoke slowly

and clearly, as befitted conversation with a chief. "*Ili kleheleche,* mighty Chief Okega-Muga. I am Gray Wolf, son of Black Oak. I bring greetings from my father and his people to you and your people."

Okega-Muga's voice was much stronger than his appearance might lead anyone to expect, and its tone indicated that the chief was not impressed by Gray Wolf's greeting. "Black Oak's lands are far from here. We not meet for many turnings of the sky." He nodded toward Susannah. "What business have you with Okega-Muga to bring this one?"

Gray Wolf stepped aside and gestured for Susannah to stand beside him.

"Su-sannah is my woman," he said. "She goes where I go."

Okega-Muga looked from Susannah to Gray Wolf and motioned to the young girl. "I smoke the pipe of peace with Black Oak's son now. Shale-ga will take the woman from this place."

"It is good, *muchomes*," Gray Wolf said. He did not look at Susannah as she followed Shale-ga from the chief's lodge.

Although Susannah had expected to be taken to the women's lodge, she would have preferred to stay and listen to the men talk, even though she might not understand all they said. For a fleeting moment, she wished that Gray Wolf had asked Okega-Muga to allow it. However, Susannah knew it would probably never occur to Gray Wolf to violate the rules by which he had lived for so long, and her request would only make matters worse between them.

It was a short distance to the women's lodge, where the unattached females of the village lived under the protection of the chief. Many were elderly, but there were a few younger girls who had apparently not yet been bound in marriage, and others of an indeterminate age that Susannah guessed were widows who had no grown children to care for them. In this village as in the others she had visited, Susannah noted that there seemed to be more women than men, no doubt a result of the years of fighting, both with other Indians and the whites.

Kentucky has its share of widows these days, too, she thought.

As Susannah entered, the women looked up from their tasks to regard her with curiosity.

"This is Su-sannah from the village of Chief Black Oak. Her man smokes the pipe with Okega-Muga."

"Ili kheleleche," Susannah said. She stood just inside the entrance until one of the oldest women, apparently the leader of the group, returned the greeting and motioned for her to sit beside her.

"I am Oletha, niece to Chief Okega-Muga. No one comes here in many days," she said. "We hear there is trouble."

As the women looked at Susannah expectantly, she realized with relief that, unlike the women in Black Oak's village, they seemed to have immediately accepted her as one of their own. Dressed much the same as they were and with their hair and coloring, Susannah's Indian heritage protected her. It was also obvious that these women were hungry for news from outside the closed world of their own village.

I wish I could tell them the truth of all that has happened to me in the past months and how God has been with me, she thought. However, she and Gray Wolf had not come so Susannah could talk about herself. It would be acceptable for her to share with them what she knew of the fate of Running Beaver and how badly Black Oak's villagers needed help, but Susannah hesitated to speak. Her lack of fluency in the Delaware language would soon be apparent, and these women might decide that she was a spy and turn against both her and Gray Wolf.

I know what angry Delaware women can do, she thought, and decided her best tactic would be to delay conversing with them for as long as she could.

"I tell you what I know, but I hunger much," Susannah said truthfully.

Oletha clapped her hands together, and instantly Shale-ga, who had sat down by the lodge door, sprang to attention and bowed. "Bring this one meat and drink," she ordered, and the girl left immediately.

❧

As tradition dictated, the pipe was smoked in silence. Several more council members appeared and joined in the ritual. When it ended, Gray Wolf sat cross-legged before Okega-Muga and waited for the chief to invite him to speak. The old man sat for many moments with his chin on his chest, appearing to be either asleep or deep in thought, before he opened his eyes and fastened them on Gray Wolf.

"Black Oak does not send his son here without a reason. What is it?"

Gray Wolf took a deep breath and touched his hand to his heart as a sign of the sincerity of what he was about to speak. "For two summers the *Shawonese* and the *schwannack* have raided Black Oak's villages. They burned our crops in the fields and took away our corn and food stores. We have no seeds to plant in the spring. Okega-Muga is a mighty chief who has much land—"

Okega-Muga's eyes flashed angrily. "Does Black Oak think that troubles have not come to this land as well? We have barely enough corn to feed our own people. There is nothing to give to Black Oak."

Gray Wolf had anticipated this initial response—it was almost expected that a first request would be turned down. He nodded before speaking again. "I know the times are harder than your people have ever known, mighty Chief. But you have many strong warriors yet, and your village still stands. Black Oak's lodges do not."

Without disputing Gray Wolf's words, Okega-Muga held his hands up, palms toward Gray Wolf in a gesture of refusal. "Running Beaver is Black Oak's kinsman. He always has much seed corn. You should go to him for help."

"My people now live in Running Beaver's village, *muchomes.*

Running Beaver and his people were gone when we got there. We do not know where they went. All their stores were burned or taken."

"It is so everywhere in the land," Okega-Muga said. "We of the Delaware that did not join the Mohawk Thayendenaga and his Mingoes and Wyandots have suffered."

"For that reason, we must help one another," Gray Wolf said. "If Okega-Muga can give us even a small sack of seed corn, he will keep our people from starving."

"I cannot give what I do not have," Okega-Muga said with an air of finality. "You will tell this to Black Oak." He turned to Exundas and spoke again. "See that Gray Wolf has food. He and his woman can stay in the council house tonight. Tomorrow he will return to his people."

The elders had listened in silence, but now they nodded and murmured their approval of Okega-Muga's words. Gray Wolf was disappointed, but he wasn't ready to give up just yet. There was still one other chance that he had to take. Black Oak had sent Su-sannah with him for more than one reason. The fact that she and Okega-Muga might be related, even distantly, might not be enough to make the chief change his mind. But it was worth a try.

"There is this other thing I would ask of you, mighty Chief."

Okega-Muga and the council looked at Gray Wolf in surprise that bordered onto shock. He had come as a stranger and been welcomed with the pipe. He had been given a chance to speak and had made his request. Even after that request had been denied, he had been offered the chief's hospitality. To ask for anything more was a dangerous violation of manners and custom.

"What is it?" asked Okega-Muga.

"Will you speak with my woman?"

"Why should I do this?" the chief asked.

The council members looked from Gray Wolf's face to Okega-Muga's, intent on their chief's reaction.

"Black Oak wants it so," Gray Wolf replied. "In his name, I ask it."

Okega-Muga was silent for a moment, then he nodded. "Bring the woman here, but be quick about it. The day grows old and I would be by the fire in my own lodge when the sun wanes."

Gray Wolf walked to Exundas, who stood by the lodge door. "Where is she?" he asked.

"In the women's lodge. I will bring her here," Exundas said.

Gray Wolf stood outside and waited for him to return with Susannah. As she approached him, Susannah raised questioning eyes to his, and Gray Wolf shook his head. When Exundas went back inside the chief's lodge, Gray Wolf spoke to Susannah with a note of urgency she had never heard before in his voice.

"The chief says he has no seeds to give to Black Oak. But he is obligated to help his kin. You must speak to him now and tell him who you are."

"What if we are not kin?" she asked.

Gray Wolf looked briefly annoyed. "Do you know that you are not?"

"I only know what my mother told me, but that was a long time ago. Okega-Muga may not remember her."

"Do not waste time in idle talk. Okega-Muga is waiting to see you."

Susannah felt a cold fear growing in the pit of her stomach. "He could say something I do not understand."

"I will tell you. Come, we go in now." Gray Wolf took Susannah's hand and led her before the place where the Chief sat.

Susannah bowed to the chief. Despite her fear, she forced herself to speak slowly and calmly. "I am Susannah, daughter of Sukeu-quawon, grand-daughter of Woakhop-sisija of the Clan of the Serpent on the Monongahela River. My mother was proud to be near kin to the great Okega-Muga. I am happy to see you, *muchomes*." she said.

Okega-Muga's expression did not change. "The Clan of the Serpent has not been on the Monongahela for many years," he said. "The women of my people stay in their lodges. They do not ride with their men. They do not speak for them."

Susannah could see a tiny muscle working in Gray Wolf's jaw and she knew he wanted to make some reply to the chief's criticism, but dared not risk their mission to do so.

"Black Oak sent us both, mighty Chief," Susannah said. "Will you hear me out?"

Okega-Muga waved his hand. "Speak what you will, then."

I don't know what to say, Susannah thought in near-panic. She brought her hand to her throat and felt the outline of her mother's cross underneath her thick deerskin dress. *Help me, God. Put the right words in my mouth.*

The soreness she felt as she pressed it against her dress reminded Susannah of the cut on her wrist. She turned the hand palm up and extended it to Okega-Muga, showing him the red line marking her wrist.

"From my mother and my grandfather I am your kin, *muchomes.* By this mark Black Oak gave me to Gray Wolf. I, Susannah, ask help in Black Oak's name for my man and his people."

When Okega-Muga said nothing, Susannah glanced at Gray Wolf with anxious eyes and wished that she was fluent enough in her mother's tongue to intercede more eloquently on behalf of Black Oak's people. Dark Moon and Dappled Faun and many others had been kind to her, and even though she could never think of herself as one of them, Susannah would not want them to starve if there were anything she could do to prevent it.

As if he understood exactly what Susannah was thinking, Gray Wolf held out his own wrist, then repeated much of what she had said and added more words of his own that she did not understand. Then he reached for her hand again and continued to hold it tightly. "My woman is proud. She does not ask this for herself, but for me and my people," he concluded.

"The People of the Serpent went to the western lands many years ago," Okega-Muga said. "How is it that you come to be in these parts?"

Susannah looked at Gray Wolf in mute appeal. She had understood Okega-Muga's question, but she feared she lacked the skill to answer it in the way that would be most diplomatic. Gray Wolf inclined his head slightly and squeezed her hand, and she knew she was to answer as well as she could.

"My father is a white hunter, *muchomes*. He and my mother live in his land."

"Schwannack!" Okega-Muga exclaimed angrily.

"No, not a bad white man," Gray Wolf said quickly.

"My father once fed the People of the Serpent in hard times," Susannah added.

"Then let her go to her father for help," Okega-Muga said. "We have no corn here."

Gray Wolf started to speak, but Susannah dug her elbow in his ribs, an action that surprised him enough to stop him before he could say more than the chief's name.

"Thank you, Chief," Susannah said, bowing deeply.

"I am sorry that I cannot help you." Okega-Muga sounded as if he meant it. "I am weary and must go to my lodge. Exundas will bring you food."

The old chief slowly made his way past them, trailed by the council members, who stared at Susannah as they passed. Gray Wolf took his hand from Susannah's and looked down at her with a sober expression. "Black Oak will not be pleased."

"I'm sorry. I tried my best—" Susannah began, but he would not let her finish.

"It is not your fault. It is because of the *schwannack* that the people will have no grain to plant in the spring."

"And the *Shawonese*," she reminded him. "They did more damage. The white soldiers did not come near your land."

"No, but when the *schwannack* burn their fields, they steal our corn. It is all the same."

"It is not the same," Susannah insisted, but before she could say more, Exundas and Shale-ga entered, carrying steaming bowls of stew and a jug of hot herbal tea.

"Okega-Muga say your horses will be fed and ready at dawn. He will not see you again."

Gray Wolf nodded. "Tell the chief we thank him. We are honored to stay in the chief's lodge."

"I will tell him. There is wood to last the night. Come, Shale-ga."

Although they had brought two bowls, Susannah took only a small portion. She had already satisfied her hunger before she had been summoned to the chief's lodge, but she welcomed the hot tea, which was quite similar to a brew that she recalled her mother making when she was a small child.

Gray Wolf began to eat immediately and said nothing until he finished the stew in his bowl and then, at Susannah's urging, ate the rest of hers.

"It is a hard thing to be hungry," he said when he finished. "It is a hard thing to tell Black Oak that there will be no corn."

"But you do not have to do this," Susannah said. From the moment that Okega-Muga had told her she must go to her white father for help, an idea had been planted that now seemed so logical that she wondered how she could have overlooked it before.

"I will not run away from my people," Gray Wolf said.

As you did, Susannah interpreted his meaning, and felt her face warm.

She looked at him steadily. "I do not ask you to. But there is seed in Kentucky. Take me there, and I will see that Black Oak gets all he needs."

ten

Gray Wolf stared at her for a moment as if he couldn't believe his ears, then his mouth twisted and he spoke bitterly. "Your man not come for you. You think I take you to him? No. I will not do this."

Susannah moved closer to Gray Wolf and put both her hands on his face, forcing him to look at her. "I have tried to tell you about my man, but you will not listen."

Gray Wolf covered her hands with his and pulled them away from his face. "I do not want to hear it," he said angrily.

"You must hear it. You can never take me to him." Susannah's voice choked with emotion. "I have no man. He is dead, killed by *Shawonese*."

Gray Wolf had continued to hold her fingers tightly, and now he held up her left hand. "You still wear his ring," he said accusingly. "You say he come for you."

"The ring is all I have left of him—and I said he would come for me to protect myself. What else could I do?"

For many months, for far too long, Susannah had tried to keep her emotions in check. With the help of the Holy Spirit, she had made her peace with God and tried not to look back on what could not be altered or changed. Until recently, she had been fairly successful at overcoming her pain. But Gray Wolf's anger was almost more than she could bear. Susannah wrenched her hands from Gray Wolf's grasp and covered her face with them. Tears spilled from her eyes and ran down her hands, and her shoulders heaved as sobs wracked her body.

In her distress, Susannah scarcely felt Gray Wolf's arms close around her as he knelt beside her and drew her close. Murmuring words too low to be understood, he rocked her in his arms as if he were comforting a hurt child. Gradually, Susannah became aware of Gray Wolf's lips brushing her forehead, the tip of her nose, and then each of her damp cheeks. Susannah opened her eyes and looked into his. There she saw her own tears reflected just before he bent to kiss her lips.

Without hesitation, Susannah returned that kiss, and then another. Gray Wolf groaned and pillowed her head on his shoulder.

"Before I see you, I think I never know love again," he said quietly.

"So did I."

"I not forget Fair Star."

"And I can never forget James. But it is wrong to worship the dead."

Gray Wolf pulled away and stared at Susannah in astonishment.

"What means to worship the dead?" he asked.

"My uncle is a man of God—the Delaware would call him *Allogagan Nehella.* He teaches that we should honor and give praise only to God and not to any of His creatures, dead or living."

Gray Wolf nodded as if he understood and stared intently at Susannah. "Was your man good to you?" he asked.

"Yes. James never wronged anyone. I loved him with all my heart," she said.

Gray Wolf pulled Susannah to him again. "So with Fair Star," he said quietly. "I think part of me die when *schwannack* kill them."

Susannah lifted her head from his chest and looked at him inquiringly. "Them?" she repeated.

Gray Wolf shuddered with the hurt of his memory. He took his arms from Susannah and wiped his eyes on his sleeve.

"Fair Star and our son," he said thickly. "He walk for the first time only the day before *schwannack* come."

Susannah put her hands on his shoulders as she set aside the memory of her own grief to comfort him in his. "I know how you feel," she said.

Gray Wolf sighed heavily. "You lose man, I lose wife and son. It is a hard thing."

"I lost a baby after my husband died," Susannah said. "In a way, that was even harder."

Gray Wolf touched his hand to her cheek. "You very brave," he said.

"No, I am not brave. For a long time after James died and I also lost his child, I thought I had no reason to live." Susannah plucked at the rawhide strand around her neck and brought the cross from beneath her deerskin dress. "But then I prayed to God and He helped me."

Gray Wolf thoughtfully traced the outlines of the cross with a finger. "You still believe in God?"

Susannah nodded. "Yes. I know He sent you to me."

"You will not run from me?"

"No. If you take me to Kentucky, I will stay with you."

Gray Wolf was quiet for a moment. Then he picked up her hand and gently kissed the faint red line on her left wrist. "Black Oak has bound us together," he said. "You now my woman."

Susannah nodded. "I know. But I would be bound in God's way, as well."

Puzzled, Gray Wolf's eyes searched hers. "How is this to be?"

Susannah touched her hand to her cross. "In Kentucky, among my people. We can be bound in the white way. Then I will really be your woman."

Gray Wolf sighed, then covered her hand with his and touched both their hands to his heart. "Here you already my woman forever, in this place or any other."

"I feel it as well, but we must also be bound in Kentucky."

"If this is what you want, it will be done."

Susannah nodded. "You have said it."

Gently Gray Wolf kissed her forehead. "We leave early tomorrow. We should sleep now." With one last, longing look at Susannah, Gray Wolf picked up his blanket and spread it on the other side of the lodge's center fire.

"Sleep will be hard this night," she said. "There is much to think about."

"No more talk," Gray Wolf warned.

Susannah smiled in the darkness. Gray Wolf had often told her not to talk, but even when she hadn't, his heart had somehow heard her.

Dear Lord, if this isn't what I was to do, please show me so now, Susannah prayed in the silence. *If Gray Wolf and I weren't supposed to fall in love, I fear it's too late—we already have. But I want us to be obedient to Your will for the future.*

Susannah thought about all that had passed between them from the moment they had first met. Surely God had already used the circumstances in which they had found themselves, and no doubt He would continue to do so.

God still has something for me to do for Gray Wolf and his people, she thought. When the time was right, Gray Wolf would regain the lost faith of his youth—for Susannah knew that he had been born into a Christian family—and together they would find the work they were meant to do.

How all that would happen would have to be the concern of another day. For now, all that mattered to Susannah was that she and Gray Wolf had at last acknowledged their love. For this night, it was enough.

Thank You, Lord, Susannah murmured.

❧

True to Okega-Muga's word, their horses were ready the next morning when, just before dawn, Susannah and Gray Wolf came out of the lodge. Exundas handed him a pouch containing jerky, parched corn, and a double handful of nuts.

"Thank the chief for his hospitality," Gray Wolf said in parting.

"Ride close and watch for the *Shawonese*," Exundas warned.

"It will be done," Gray Wolf said.

"What was that about watching for Shawnees?" Susannah asked when they had passed through the sleeping village and were safely out of earshot. "The weather grows cold. Surely Shawnees do not still raid."

"Some do. The *schwannak* took their food. They must take other tribes' food."

Susannah looked around her as if she expected a Shawnee to pop out from behind every tree. "Do you fear them?" she asked.

Gray Wolf shrugged. "A man cannot live always in fear. If *Shawonese* come, they come. But we not see them on the way to Okega-Muga. I do not think we see them on the way home."

Home. Susannah's heart contracted at Gray Wolf's use of the word. To him, home was the place where Black Oak and his people lived, no matter what stream it might lie beside or how many times the people might have to move their village over the years. To Susannah, however, home meant nothing at the moment. She had lived only briefly in Kentucky, and while she wanted to go back there to let Hannah and Nate know she was all right and to get the supplies Black Oak's people needed, she had no desire to remain there. She would also like to see her father and the rest of her family in North Carolina, but she wouldn't want to stay there permanently. In fact, Susannah could not imagine living anywhere apart from Gray Wolf.

I am your man now, he had told her. When they reached Kentucky and were married, both legally and in the sight of God who had brought them together, then they could consider where and how they should live.

In the meantime, they faced a long trip back to Running Beaver's village.

"I hope you are right," Susannah said.

Gray Wolf half-smiled and reached over to cover her hand with his. "I have said it," he said. "The way is long. No more talk now."

They saw no sign of anyone else on the trail for the rest of the day. When the sun stood straight overhead, Gray Wolf stopped and divided the food that Exundas had given them, saving part of it for the evening. When the evening shadows began to darken to purple, Gray Wolf motioned that they would make camp for the night in the woods to the side of the trail.

There were no convenient cabins along the way he had chosen as their return route, but there were white oak trees, and with his tomahawk Gray Wolf quickly cut many strips of their bark. Then he dug two holes, each roughly the size of a small cooking pot, each near a tree, before criss-crossing the wood strips atop the hole and igniting them with flint and steel.

"What are you doing?" Susannah asked, thinking that one larger fire would seem more sensible than two smaller ones.

"Watch. You see," Gray Wolf replied. As soon as the bark strips were glowing, he covered the pit with the earth he had dug out, leaving only two small vent holes. "Sit here," he ordered.

Gray Wolf gestured that she was to lean back against the tree, then he showed her how to cover her head and the glowing fire with a blanket. "You stay warm this way. We eat now," Gray Wolf said.

With night falling in the forest, they sat in companionable silence with their blankets around their shoulders and shared the rest of the food from Okega-Muga's village.

"This little fire is warm," Susannah said after a while.

Gray Wolf nodded. "White oak makes no smoke, tell no *Shawonese* where we are."

"My father also knows such things," Susannah said.

"He not teach you?" Gray Wolf asked.

"No. There was no need. In Carolina, we did not live in the

woods."

"Then where he hunt?"

Susannah made an inclusive gesture. "All over—the west of Virginia and Pennsylvania, the Ken-tuck lands—up in the Ohio at least once."

"My first father hunted, too," Gray Wolf said.

It was the first time that Susannah had any inkling that Gray Wolf recalled any father except Black Oak, and she waited for him to continue. When he did not, she spoke. "You must remember him, then."

Gray Wolf shook his head. "Not much—a big man with eyes the color of the sky and deep voice. We go in canoe for many days, get much beaver pelts."

He fell silent again, and sensing that he might be reliving the painful tragedy that had taken him from his parents, Susannah laid her hand gently on his. "Then what happened?" she prompted.

Gray Wolf hung his head and sighed. "The *schwannack* come,"he said flatly. "They talk, they eat. They have knives, they have rifles. They—"

Gray Wolf broke off talking, but Susannah finished for him. "The *schwannack* killed your mother and your father. They took their beaver pelts and left. How did you get away?"

His voice was tense with anger as he spoke again. "I in woods when they come and they not know I see them. They laugh, they take canoe with pelts. I want to run after them, I want to kill them. I not do it. I do nothing."

Tears of compassion welled in Susannah's eyes as she reached over to put her arms around Gray Wolf and hold him tightly for a moment. "You were only a child. There was nothing you could do," she said, knowing that the scene of his parents' murder must have haunted him though the years.

"I run into the woods," Gray Wolf said as if reliving the experience afresh. "I fall down, scratch arms. I not know where

I go. I not see the *schwannack* again."

"Then Black Oak found you?" Susannah questioned.

"No—Dark Moon. I run from her, too, but she follow me. She say she take me to place where no *schwannack* will ever come for me."

Imagining the scene, Susannah thought it was no wonder that he ran from Dark Moon; the woman must have frightened him almost as much as the white men who had wantonly killed his parents for the pelts his father had gathered.

"She saved your life," Susannah said.

Gray Wolf nodded. "She did same later for Fair Star."

"And for me, as well," Susannah said. "She saved me from some of the village women while you were away."

"Dark Moon not tell me this," Gray Wolf said. "She tell me you go away to bring much *schwannack* to kill Black Oak's people."

Susannah touched her hand to his again. "You know this is not so," she said.

"We go to Ken-tucky, *schwannack* follow us back."

Susannah shook her head vigorously. "No, it will not happen. My people will see that it does not."

"Black Oak will not know this," Gray Wolf said.

"You will tell him. The people must have seed corn. We must go to Kentucky."

"Not this night." Gray Wolf kissed each of Susannah's cheeks, then her forehead. "Sleep now. This trouble is later."

Susannah murmured a goodnight as Gray Wolf pulled the blanket up around her head and she rested against the broad tree trunk.

Gray Wolf might not yet be able to quote the thirty-fourth verse of the Gospel of Matthew, but he had learned its lesson well, she thought. *Take therefore no thought for the morrow: for the morrow shall take thought for the things of itself. Sufficient unto the day is the evil thereof.*

Yet Susannah had also been taught that there was another way to look at that verse of Scripture. Sufficient unto each day, also, is the goodness thereof. *God, please bring to us both days filled with goodness and mercy,* she prayed.

❧

They reached the village at mid-afternoon the next day, just as a cold rain that had been falling for several hours gave way to light snow. They had talked very little the whole day, but the closer they came to Black Oak's village, the more apprehensive Gray Wolf seemed to become. Susannah knew it would not be easy for him to tell his father that their mission had failed, and even harder for him to ask permission to take Susannah across the river.

Black Oak came out of his lodge to meet them, but did not invite them inside.

"Is he angry?" Susannah asked, when after the briefest of greetings, Black Oak turned his back on them.

"No. He knows we have long ride. He speak to us after we rest and eat."

"Us?" Susannah repeated. "Black Oak will see me, too?"

Gray Wolf looked almost surprised. "He sent you as well as me. It is right you tell him your part. Now, no more talk," he said. "Let us find food."

Susannah hadn't seen Dark Moon until she suddenly seemed to materialize beside them. "It is good that you come back," she said.

Immediately, Susannah noticed that something seemed different about Dark Moon. The old woman had pulled her hair back from her face with a beaded headband and replaced her moth-eaten buffalo robe with a handsome cloak made from turkey feathers. Apparently Gray Wolf noticed the change, too, for he asked Dark Moon what had happened to her in their absence.

The old woman shrugged. "You will hear of it in time. Go

now to your lodge. I have sent food there for you," she said, then walked away without a backward glance.

"Dark Moon looks like a different person," Susannah said. "She seems to have her wits about her now."

"Sometimes things from long time back trouble her," Gray Wolf said.

As they do us all, Susannah thought. But she intended to look ahead, not into the well of her past woe.

"I am hungry," she said instead. "Let's see what Dark Moon brought us."

&

It had grown dark, and snow still fell as Susannah and Gray Wolf walked hand-in-hand to the council lodge. A hot meal and brief rest had done much to restore Susannah's spirits. While she did not look forward to having to tell Black Oak that their mission had failed, she felt confident that it would lead the way to her return to Kentucky.

"I talk now," Gray Wolf said as they reached the lodge entrance. "You talk when I say."

Susannah nodded and smiled encouragingly at him. Gray Wolf looked as if he would like to kiss her, but instead he dropped her hand and pushed aside the door-flap to enter the lodge.

The full council had gathered to hear Gray Wolf's report, and after the usual rituals of greeting, all watched with interest as he and Susannah stood before Black Oak and Gray Wolf began to speak.

"Okega-Muga sends his greetings and those of his people to the mighty Black Oak and the people of his village. Okega-Muga and his people have had many troubles. The *Shawonese* have taken their seed corn. There is none to give to Black Oak's people."

Black Oak listened impassively, then turned to Susannah. "How is it that you do not claim a kinsman's share?"

"She did, *muchomes*," Gray Wolf said quickly. "Okega-Muga knows that Su-sannah is his kin. He cannot give what he does not have."

"This is hard," Black Oak murmured. "Our people need corn."

"They will have it, father. Okega-Muga tell us where to get help."

Black Oak furrowed his brow. "What does Okega-Muga say?" he asked.

"He says he cannot help Su-sannah, but she has other kin that will."

Black Oak looked at Susannah in surprise. "Is this so?"

Susannah nodded. "Yes, *muchomes*." She looked at Gray Wolf, her eyes urging him to tell Black Oak what she feared she lacked the ability to say as well.

Black Oak shook his head. "The Clan of the Serpent is beyond the great river. It is too far."

"We not go there, my father. Su-sannah has closer kin beyond the Ohio, in Ken-tucky."

"Ken-tucky!" Black Oak's voice was heavy with contempt. "No Lenni-Lenape live in that land. Since the *schwannack* come, we cannot even hunt there. No one there gives Black Oak seed corn."

"My kin will help," Susannah said earnestly. "It is so."

"Do you know this that your woman says?" Black Oak asked Gray Wolf.

"Yes, *muchomes*. There is much seed corn in Ken-tucky. She has said it."

"Ken-tucky not safe for Gray Wolf and his woman. *Schwannack* there have much rifles," Black Oak said firmly.

"They will not harm us," Susannah said.

Running Fox rose from his council seat and stood between Black Oak and Gray Wolf. "Do not listen, Father! The woman will bring *schwannack* to kill us all."

Black Oak seemed annoyed at the interruption, but he ignored his son. He looked into Susannah's eyes as if trying to
decide if he could believe her words. "Leave us now," he said
to her at length. "We will speak of this thing."

"As you say, *muchomes*." Susannah bowed to Black Oak,
gave Gray Wolf a half-smile, then brushed past Running Fox
and walked out into the swirling snow and back to the lodge
she would share with Gray Wolf as long as they stayed in Black
Oak's village.

Susannah was aware that she and Gray Wolf would have
great difficulty trying to get to Kentucky on their own, without
Black Oak's horses or approval. But as she waited for Gray
Wolf to return, Susannah knew that they must go, with or without the chief's approval.

Dear Lord, please help Gray Wolf say the right words, she
prayed.

Susannah opened her eyes to see Dark Moon standing in the
lodge doorway.

"Okega-Muga not give you seed corn," Dark Moon said,
making it a statement.

"He has none to give," Susannah said. "We must go to Kentucky for help."

"What says Black Oak about this?" Dark Moon asked.

"I do not know. They talk of it now."

"Gray Wolf will do what you want. He goes to Kentucky
with you."

"How do you know this?" Susannah asked.

Dark Moon lowered herself to sit beside Susannah and
pointed to the mark of their binding on her wrist. "Gray Wolf
is your man. He will do as you say."

Susannah smiled faintly. "He would not like to hear you say
this."

The old woman shrugged. "I see the way he look at you. He
will go. I will ask my man about this."

Susannah looked at Dark Moon in surprise, not sure that she had heard her correctly. "You have a man?"

Dark Moon stroked the soft turkey feathers of her new cloak and looked pleased with herself, then touched her beaded headband. "He give me these," she said.

Susannah tried without success to recall ever seeing any of the village men anywhere near Dark Moon. "Who is this man?"

The old woman chuckled as she walked to the door. "You find out soon," she said. "Keep the fire fed. This night will be cold."

After Dark Moon left, Susannah thought about the secret identity of Dark Moon's man and wondered what was happening in the council lodge. She had just put a few more sticks of wood on the fire when Gray Wolf finally returned to the lodge. Susannah stood and searched his impassive face in vain for a clue to Black Oak's decision.

Gray Wolf took Susannah into his arms and kissed her. "Running Fox angry. He not like this," he said.

Susannah pulled away to look at Gray Wolf. "Running Fox is not chief. What does Black Oak say?"

Gray Wolf gave Susannah a rare, brief smile before he bent to kiss her lightly. "Black Oak say we come to the council house tomorrow. He tell us then," he said.

Susannah's disappointment was written on her face. "I hoped he would tell you tonight. Why does he make us wait?"

"Black Oak wants all to know what is to be done."

"I suppose that is best," Susannah said. "But I wish I already knew we would go to Kentucky."

"You do," Gray Wolf said, and his expression told her that Dark Moon had been right—Gray Wolf would take her there, whether or not Black Oak officially approved.

Once more Susannah felt her heart lift in appreciation of this strange white Indian who had given her his love and protection.

Thank You, God, she prayed.

For the first time, Susannah felt a warm assurance that, no matter what might happen the next day, the Holy Spirit would continue to work in her life in ways that she could never dream possible.

eleven

When she awoke the next morning, Susannah was not surprised to find that Gray Wolf had already left the lodge. From their very first meeting, Gray Wolf had always been careful to allow her privacy. Now, even though they shared his dwelling, Gray Wolf did his best to keep his distance. Susannah appreciated his consideration, but from the moment she knew that he loved her, Susannah felt that a part of her was missing when they were separated, and she was always relieved to see him again.

Hearing someone at the lodge entrance, Susannah turned with an eager smile, expecting to see Gray Wolf. Instead, Dappled Faun entered, holding a new, almost-white doeskin garment decorated with fringe and several rows of beads.

"You are to put this on, then Dark Moon waits to see you," Dappled Faun said.

"Where is Gray Wolf?" Susannah asked.

"He is already at the council lodge. Hurry."

While Dappled Faun waited for her at the door, Susannah slipped into the new dress, which felt soft and warm. She put a blanket shawl-fashion around her shoulders and stepped outside. Immediately her feet plunged into several inches of wet snow, and despite her heavy moccasins, Susannah felt the cold and damp numbing her feet.

"You need leggings," Dappled Faun observed as Susannah floundered on through the snow. Her own feet were wrapped in what appeared to be a double layer of deerskin, topped by rawhide leggings that ended somewhere under her long deerskin shift.

"I did not know it was so cold," Susannah said.

"It is warm in Dark Moon's lodge," Dappled Faun said.

Dark Moon sat by the fire, wearing an elaborately-beaded dress similar to the one that Dappled Faun had just brought Susannah. She motioned for Susannah to sit beside her. "This is the last time we meet in this lodge,"she said. "It may be last chance to speak together."

Surprised, Susannah looked at the old woman and wondered if her madness might have returned. Certainly her words made no sense. "Why do you say this?" Susannah asked.

Dark Moon glanced down and smoothed the heavy fringe adorning her dress. "Tomorrow you and Gray Wolf will go away. Nothing ever be the same again."

"How do you know this?" Susannah asked. "Did Black Oak speak of it?"

Dark Moon looked amused. "The chief does not tell me this, but I know it will be so. When Gray Wolf leave him last night he had not decided. I tell Black Oak that you have gold and can buy much seed corn in Ken-tucky. Now he must let you go."

Susannah felt as if the breath had been knocked out of her. "This is not a good thing for all to know of the gold," she managed to say after a moment.

"Only Black Oak hears it," she said. "You will see."

"I hope you are right," Susannah answered.

"There will be a ceremony this day. After it, I come no more to this lodge." Dark Moon said.

Susannah looked at Dark Moon's elaborate dress and re-membered what she had said about her man giving her the turkey-feather cloak. Suddenly she realized what Dark Moon must be trying to tell her.

"You are to be bound to the chief?" she asked, and Dark Moon laughed in delight at Susannah's surprise and tapped her temple with her forefinger.

"Many think that he the crazy one," she said. Then her expression grew serious and her voice softened. "Black Oak is lonely in his lodge since the mother of Running Fox die. He needs woman to care for him."

"Will he cut your wrist?" Susannah asked.

"No. You cut because you not bound by blood before." Dark Moon pointed to a faint scar in the fold of her wrist. "I have this done many years ago."

"You have not told me how you came to be here," Susannah said.

Dark Moon shook her head. "I do not know. *Shawonese* killed my children and left me for dead. These people took me in and made me blood daughter to Chief Tall Trees. I will not be cut again."

Acting on an impulse, Susannah pulled the rawhide necklace from underneath her dress and untied it. She removed the gold band that James had placed on her hand a lifetime ago and held it out to Dark Moon. "Take this as the sign of your binding."

Dark Moon's eyes glittered. "I give it back to you once. It is yours."

"No, you must have it. I will never wear it again." Susannah thrust the ring into Dark Moon's hand and closed her fingers around it. "You have done much for me—and for Gray Wolf."

Dark Moon nodded solemnly. "It is good gift," she said. "I give you rabbit skins to line your moccasins. The way to Kentucky is long and cold."

"Thank you, Dark Moon." Blinking back threatening tears, Susannah leaned over to hug the old woman. "Soon we will meet again."

"It may be so. But now we must go to the council lodge. Black Oak not like me to be late for this binding."

❧

Gray Wolf waited for Susannah near the entrance, and she was pleased to see how his eyes lit up when he saw her. "You like the dress?" he asked, and she knew then that he must have sent it to her.

Was it Fair Star's? The thought crossed Susannah's mind, but she immediately dismissed it. What if it had been? Fair Star belonged in the past, as did James. Gray Wolf was her man now, and that was all that mattered.

Susannah smiled at Gray Wolf. "It is beautiful," she said.

He took her hand and led her to stand beside Black Oak. There was an air of excitement as the drum was brought out and several young men, barefoot despite the snow outside, began a slow, rhythmical dance. Just as it ended, the door-flap opened and Dark Moon entered. In the turkey-feather cloak that topped the new beaded dress, she bore little resemblance to the crazed woman who more than once had bent the entire village to her will.

All eyes watched Dark Moon make her way slowly to Black Oak and bow.

The chief reached his right hand to her left hand and brought her to stand beside him. He began a low, melodious chant, punctuated by the drum. Susannah looked at Gray Wolf and remembered that not so long ago, such a chant had bound them in the same way.

Black Oak finished his chant and spoke, his voice stronger than Susannah had ever heard it. While she couldn't make out all the words, she distinctly heard him say that the woman Dark Moon would now move into his lodge.

Dark Moon held up her hand, showing the ring that now adorned her little finger. Black Oak gaped at it in surprise as a shout of approval went up from the gathered villagers, and the ceremony was over.

"Did you know of this binding?" she asked Gray Wolf.

"No, but my father's lodge was lonely. It is good he does this."

Dark Moon sat cross-legged on the ground beside her new husband, and Black Oak raised his hands for quiet. He began to speak of their need for seed corn and to repeat what they already knew—that Gray Wolf and Susannah had asked for help.

"Chief Okega-Muga say his people have no seed corn to give us."

The people's festive mood had begun to change when Black Oak spoke of their need for seed corn, but now their disappointment verged onto anger as they murmured among themselves. Several of the villagers, both men and women, looked at Susannah as if the failure of their mission was probably her fault. Once more Black Oak had to raise his hands for quiet.

"The people will have seed corn in time to plant. The woman Su-sannah and my son Gray Wolf will go to Ken-tucky and bring seed back to us."

Susannah felt a great sense of relief and smiled at Gray Wolf. He did not return her smile, but squeezed Susannah's hand.

"Ken-tucky!" The word was on many lips at once as the villagers looked at each other in disbelief.

"The *schwannack* will kill them. They will never let them bring seed corn to us," muttered one of the warriors who had gone on the flatboat raid.

Black Oak looked levelly at the speaker. "It is not your risk," he said loudly. "I have spoken—they go."

He addressed Gray Wolf. "We cannot spare two horses. You and Su-sannah must ride together. You may take food to sustain you to the river. No more."

"Thank you, *muchomes*," Gray Wolf said. "All will be done as you say."

Black Oak lowered his voice to make sure that no one overheard him. "I will see that Running Fox and others keep busy this day. You must leave soon."

"Yes, Father." Gray Wolf touched his hand to his heart, a

gesture which Susannah repeated. Maybe women weren't supposed to do it, but she wanted Black Oak to know she appreciated his trust.

As if her gesture had reminded him of something, Black Oak pointed to the narrow strip of rawhide around her neck. "Dark Moon say you wear sign. I would see it."

Susannah glanced at Dark Moon, who stared straight ahead as if she wanted to have no part in what was to follow. She lifted the rawhide necklace over her head and held it out to Black Oak. "My father made this for Sukeu-quawon when he lived with the Clan of the Serpent," Susannah said. "It showed her people that she followed Christ."

Much as Gray Wolf had done, Black Oak touched the wooden cross and then hastily withdrew his hand as if he feared it might harm him. "I will keep it until you bring the corn," he said.

"Do not do this, Father," Gray Wolf said with some urgency. "Let Su-sannah have her cross."

"No. It's all right," Susannah said steadily. Although she would mourn its loss, she knew that Black Oak wanted a tangible sign that she and Gray Wolf would carry out their mission. "I will take it back when we return."

"It will be done, my daughter." Susannah felt an unexpected surge of affection for the chief. For the first time he had called her his daughter, and in a strange way she felt that she was.

When we return I will speak to him of the way Christ died on a cross for all our sin, she promised herself.

"I am sorry about the cross," Gray Wolf said when they reached their lodge again.

Susannah touched the spot below her throat where she was accustomed to feeling its reassuring outline. "It only reminds me of my faith. I do not need it for God to help us get to Kentucky."

"May it be so, then. Come, there much to do."

While Gray Wolf saw to saddling their horse and gathering their provisions, Susannah exchanged her new doeskin dress for the only garment left from her former life, a blue homespun dress that hung on her now much thinner frame. On top of it Susannah put the deerskin shift that Dark Moon had given her. When they reached Kentucky, she could remove it and unbraid her hair and her appearance would attract no attention. As for Gray Wolf, since most frontiersmen dressed in buckskins and some even braided their hair, there was little he needed to do to change his appearance. However, a man like Gray Wolf would likely attract attention wherever he went, especially from the ladies.

Getting to Kentucky may be only half the battle, Susannah thought. But first, they had to get across the Ohio River.

Help us find the way, she prayed.

ða

It was cloudy and still spitting snow when Gray Wolf and Susannah left their lodge. No one paid them any attention as they walked into the woods, where their horse stood, saddled and waiting. Gray Wolf boosted Susannah onto the animal's wide rump, then swung into the saddle and slapped the reins. Without a single farewell from anyone, they left the village that now depended upon them for its future.

As the day wore on, more wet snow began to fall, and Susannah unrolled her blanket and covered both their heads with it.

"I wish the snow would stop," she complained.

"No, it is good," Gray Wolf replied. "No one comes out on a day like this. We travel safe."

"Yes, if we don't freeze," she murmured, but if Gray Wolf heard her, he made no reply.

Although they soon reached the Ohio shore, at that point the river was far too deep and broad to cross. In silence Gray Wolf rode east along the shore for a long way, searching for shoals they could ford. Just as darkness was about to overtake them, Gray Wolf found a likely place and decided it was better to go ahead and try to cross, rather than wait until the next day, when dawn and better weather might also bring out a number of other travelers.

"Hold up your feet and hang on to me," Gray Wolf said. Lashing the reins across the reluctant horses's withers, he urged the animal forward into the cold rushing water.

"Oh!" exclaimed Susannah when the horse slipped on some rocks, tilting her sideways until she thought they must surely go down in the water, horse and all. She had already had one swim in the winter-cold Ohio River; she feared she might not survive another. But then the animal recovered, and although their clothing was soaked all the way up to their knees, they managed to reach the Kentucky side without any other mishap.

Gray Wolf dismounted and helped Susannah down, then led the horse into a grove of hardwoods. "Now we can rest," Gray Wolf said. "There is white oak here—I will make us trail fires."

As he had on the way back from Okega-Muga's village, Gray Wolf dug two fire pits and set up individual fires for them. When their clothes had dried and they had eaten of the food Black Oak furnished them, Susannah noticed that Gray Wolf seemed unusually quiet and reflective.

I know why, Susannah thought. *We are in the Kentucky lands now, and soon Gray Wolf will be among the white people that he hates so much. It will be hard for him.*

"It will not be easy for me to see my people again," Susannah said aloud. "They probably think that I am dead, and I know I do not look the same as I did when I left them."

Gray Wolf looked at her curiously. "You never say why you leave."

"I wanted to go to my father in Carolina," Susannah said, then she paused. "No, I really wanted to leave Kentucky. My cousin is to have a baby very soon and I did not want to be reminded of the child I lost."

"They make you stay in Kentucky," he said.

"No. They are good people."

"They are white," Gray Wolf muttered in Delaware, and Susannah pretended not to hear him.

To herself, Susannah acknowledged that both Nate and Hannah McIntyre were white, and that Nate had pursued Indians far into the Ohio lands. But they had no blind hatred of all Indians, and Susannah was certain they would not stand in the way of her happiness. And now, more than ever, Susannah was convinced that to be happy, she must be with Gray Wolf.

"We will likely start meeting people on the trail tomorrow," she said aloud. "You need a white-sounding name."

"My first name was Bill," he said.

"Do you recall your last name?" Susannah asked, but he shook his head.

"I will call you Bill Gray, then. But if we meet anyone, I will do the talking."

Gray Wolf nodded. "It is so with all women," he said with mock seriousness.

Susannah imitated Gray Wolf. "No more talk. It is late and I am tired."

Gray Wolf kissed her cheek and adjusted her blanket. "Sleep now. I will watch for a while."

&

"I hear wolf howl, but I see no one," Gray Wolf told Susannah the next morning, and she knew that he must have kept a sleepless vigil.

"The snow is melting," she observed. "It must be warmer."

They rode for many miles without seeing anyone else. Occasionally they sighted smoke from a cabin off in the distance, and once a single rider passed them, going somewhere in such a hurry that he barely yelled out a "Hallo" in greeting.

The trail on which they rode was already deeply rutted from the wheels of settlers' ox-carts and wagons. In only a few years, the narrow traces made by buffalo seeking salt licks had widened to thoroughfares that split the wilderness and had doomed it to extinction.

"Do you know where you go?" Gray Wolf asked Susannah when she bade him to head the horse into a narrower and more easterly trail.

"We will be there soon."

As darkness began to fall, the road widened, and they saw a stockade fence in the distance. Susannah knew that behind it lay a handful of cabins.

"That's McClelland's Station," she said. "My cousin's homestead is not much farther."

A ghostly moon suffused the countryside with light and silvered the trace leading to the McIntyre's cabin. A welcome plume of smoke appeared on the horizon, and with anticipation mixed with apprehension, Susannah knew that she would soon face Hannah and Nate.

What will they think of me? Susannah wondered. She knew she had changed a great deal in the weeks she had been with the people of Black Oak's village, due in large part to the white Indian to whom she had given her heart.

Susannah had left Kentucky in grief, mindful only of herself and her losses. She now returned to seek help for Black Oak's people—*My people,* Susannah amended.

Lord, help me make Hannah and Nate understand, she prayed.

As they neared the house, a chorus of dogs began barking. Almost immediately the cabin door opened a cautious crack and the barrel of a rifle glinted in the moonlight. Immediately Gray Wolf reined in the horse and reached for his rifle.

"No—that's just Nate," Susannah said quickly.

"Who goes there?" a voice called from the cabin.

Susannah slid from the horse and stood where she could be clearly seen. "It's me, Nate—Susannah. I've come back to Kentucky."

The door opened wider. Still aiming the rifle toward them, a tall, slender man stood silhouetted against the light of the fireplace behind him. "Ye on the horse—stay where ye are!" Nate warned. "The woman can come closer."

Gray Wolf grasped the hunting knife in his waistband. "I do not like this white man's greeting," he said in a low voice.

"He has need to be careful," Susannah said. "Wait here—it will be all right when he sees me."

At Susannah's approach, Nate lowered his rifle. When she came near enough for him to make out her features, he cried out and stepped forward to embrace her in a bear hug. His voice shook with emotion as he stood back and stared at her. "It really is ye! But we heard that ye were dead!"

"I feared you might believe so," Susannah said. She looked past Nate to the cabin behind him. "Is Hannah all right?"

"Aye, she's inside." Nate warily nodded toward Gray Wolf, who had dismounted and stood watching them in silence. "And who is this man?"

Many times in the past few days Susannah had rehearsed how she would introduce Gray Wolf and explain how they had come to be together. She had intended to call him "Bill" and only gradually fill in the details of their relationship. But now that they were actually in Kentucky and she faced Nate McIntyre, Susannah rejected that plan.

Susannah turned and beckoned to Gray Wolf, who slowly walked to her. She took his hand in hers and held it tightly, taking new strength from the man she loved. Prompted by the same Holy Spirit who had led her back to Kentucky, Susannah suddenly knew the words she must say.

"This is Gray Wolf. He saved my life and I intend to marry him as soon as a wedding can be arranged."

Nate's jaw fell open in astonishment, and for once the usually talkative man seemed to be speechless. He glanced at Gray Wolf, then back to Susannah. "In this moonlight he looks almost white," Nate said.

"Gray Wolf is white," Susannah said. "Or at least, his parents were."

"You need not speak for me," Gray Wolf said stiffly.

Bewildered, Nate shook his head. "I'm sorry, lass. I've not got over the shock of seein' that ye really do live, much less that ye've come back with a man."

"Will you invite us inside?" Susannah prompted.

"Of course, lass. Go warm yourself. I'll see to the horse."

"I go with you," Gray Wolf said. He followed Nate to the lean-to stable behind the double cabin, and Susannah went inside.

"What is it? Why were the dogs barking?" a muffled voice called from the bedroom.

Susannah went to the doorway and spoke into the darkness. "Don't be afraid, Hannah. The dogs were just welcoming me."

There was a short silence, then Hannah let out a loud exclamation of joy. "Susannah? Can that really be you? Bring a light. I want to make sure I'm not dreaming."

Susannah found a candle on the mantle and bent to light it from the fireplace. She took it into the bedroom and set it on a small bedside table. Hannah sat up on the side of the bed, her eyes wide in wonder.

"How are you?" Susannah asked.

Hannah put a hand on her huge belly and smiled ruefully. "As well as I will be until I bear this child, if I ever do. But never mind me—where have you been all this time? We heard you were dead."

Susannah sat on the bed beside Hannah and hugged her shoulders. "'Tis a long story," she said. "Who told you I was dead?"

Remembering, Hannah sighed heavily. "A river traveler came on a half-burned flatboat and found one of the Hunter boys hiding in the cane nearby, half-dead from the cold. He brought the lad to Lexington, and Mary Chandler sent one of the Yarrows out to tell Nate. They went to the place where the boy said the Indians attacked, but found nothing."

"I had long been in Indian Territory by then," Susannah said.

"You've lost weight, and you sound different, too," Hannah commented. "It must have been an awful time. But thank God you're back!"

"I do thank God," Susannah said softly.

Tomorrow they would talk more. She would ask Nate to help her use some of her gold coins to buy seed corn for Black Oak's people, and they would ride into Lexington and find a minister to marry them, and all that happened would be because the Holy Spirit had heard Susannah's groanings when she did not know what to pray for herself.

Nate McIntyre entered the room in time to hear his wife's remark and Susannah's response to it. "And so should we all thank Him right now," he declared, and Hannah and Susannah held hands and bowed their heads as Nate began to pray.

Behind him, Gray Wolf stood in the doorway and watched them. With a tumult of feelings churning inside him, he remembered the way his first father had also stood and lifted his face to heaven in prayer. He had a vague memory of a soft, kind woman who had folded his hands together and taught him to ask God's blessings as he fell asleep each night.

That had been long, long ago, and until he met Susannah, he had all but forgotten the God in whom the white boy named Bill had put his childish trust.

I want to believe in God and His Son, Jesus. I want this faith that Susannah and her people have. Tears came to Gray Wolf's eyes, and by the time Nate McIntyre's prayer had ended with a loud "Amen," a peace that Gray Wolf had never known filled him.

Now I can pray, too, he thought with a kind of wonder, and thanked his God that it was so.

twelve

Susannah began telling her story after breakfast the next morning, and it took several hours to finish. Gray Wolf sat close beside her, and occasionally he corrected or added something to her narrative, but for the most part he remained silent.

"Black Oak's people must have seed corn or they will starve. That is why we came here. I hope you will help us, Nate," she finished.

Nate and Hannah had also listened to Susannah in silence, asking only an occasional question, their faces betraying little of what they thought. Now, however, Nate frowned and shook his head. "Ye tell me that these people raided the flatboat and killed all the Hunters save one, and ye would also ha'e died but for the grace of God. Why should we help such people?"

Gray Wolf's face reddened at Nate's words. "My people raid because the *Shawonese* and the *schwannack* take away their food. My people not raid if they have food."

"Can ye guarantee it?" Nate asked.

Gray Wolf looked questioningly at Susannah. "What is guaran-tee?" he asked.

"Nate wants to be sure that no more raids will be made against white people."

Gray Wolf spread his hands and shrugged. "I have said it," he said.

"Black Oak does not hate white people. In fact, he just married a white woman," Susannah said. "I am sure he will not raid if his people can be properly fed and clothed."

Nate sighed. "That may be true, but ye need money to buy seed corn. If Black Oak has nothing to trade, he can get nothing in return."

Susannah touched her waist as if to reassure herself that the coins were still safe. "I still have my gold, enough for much seed," she said. "I will buy what is needed myself if you won't help me."

Nate smiled ruefully and shook his head. "Ye've been too long with the Delaware, Susannah. Ye now talk just like your mother."

"I hope you mean that as a compliment," Susannah said. "I can think of nothing I would like more than to be like my mother.

"Susannah, you know Nate meant no harm," Hannah said quickly.

"Hannah's right. I thought highly of your mother and I was happy for my friend Jonny McKay when he wed her. But her Clan of the Serpent never came raiding amongst the whites like Black Oak's tribe."

"They will not do it again," Susannah repeated. "It is settled——Gray Wolf and I will ride into Lexington and find a merchant who will sell us seed corn. Then we'll find a minister to marry us and be on our way back across the Ohio and trouble you no more."

"Oh, don't take on so, Susannah," Hannah said. "Nate'll get the seed for you and find you a minister, too, but don't be in such a hurry to leave us again."

Hannah's gentle admonition shamed Susannah into a half-apology. "We'll stay here awhile, but the people will need stores soon. I would not have them raid again because they had no other choice."

Hannah smiled at Gray Wolf, then looked at Nate as if she expected him to agree. "I understand. I am sure my husband will be glad to help your people."

"It is good," Gray Wolf murmured.

Nate looked closely at him. "Susannah said you don't remember much about your white parents."

Gray Wolf nodded. "It is so. I only small boy when whites kill them."

Nate stroked his beard, a sign that he was thinking. "That must have been fifteen years or so ago. Jon McKay and I were still hunting in those days. I remember meeting a fellow named Ezra McBride who had his wife and son with him. We made camp together. His wife and the lad both had the bluest eyes I ever saw, and I recall thinkin' that he was puttin' them both in danger, takin' them so far into the wilderness."

"Do you remember the boy's name?" Susannah asked.

"I believe his ma called him Billy," Nate said. He looked at Gray Wolf again. "'Tis a long time since then and I've no way to know for sure, but ye could be that very lad. And even if ye're not, likely your father was a lonely trapper who wanted his family wi' him."

Gray Wolf was silent for a moment, then briefly inclined his head.

"It is good to know," he said. He pointed to the Bible that held a place of honor on the McIntyre table. "My mother had book like that," he said unexpectedly. "She said stories to me from it but I do not know them now."

Susannah put her hand on Gray Wolf's and laid her head briefly on his shoulder. She looked over at Nate. "His life has not been easy."

"I do not say this," Gray Wolf said quickly.

"Ye know of the Bible," Nate said. "Can ye read it?"

Gray Wolf shook his head. "No. But I would like to know the words. Su-sannah tell me some of the stories."

"I can teach you to read," said Susannah, and wondered why Gray Wolf had never said that he wanted to learn. "In Lexington, there are books."

"We will not stay there," Gray Wolf said, almost making it a question.

"No. We go to Lexington for seed corn and the books and the marrying, but we do not stay there," Susannah said.

"Oh!" Hannah cried out in sudden surprise. She clutched her side and looked at Susannah. "I think there might be another reason for you to go to Lexington," she said. "I may soon have need of the midwife there."

Nate sprang to his feet and looked at Susannah and Gray Wolf. "We'll go right away!" he exclaimed.

"And leave Hannah here alone?" Susannah regarded him with amusement. "It will yet be some hours before much happens. Gray Wolf and I can go to Lexington now. Tell me where to find the midwife, and I'll send her on."

Nate pulled on his beard in agitation. "Ask at Mary Chandler's—'tis some woman she knows."

"I suppose Mary can direct us to a minister, as well," Susannah said.

"Yes, we could all use some prayers." Nate said, then looked puzzled when both his wife and Susannah laughed.

"She means to find a minister to marry them, husband," Hannah said. Then she gasped as another pain struck her.

"Maybe Nate should go for the midwife and let me stay here with you," Susannah said. "I don't want to miss anything," she added lightly, but she was concerned that Hannah's pains, while barely underway, already seemed to be coming so close together.

Nate looked relieved. "I'm sorry to be the cause of disturbin' your plans, but it'll ease my mind to have ye here."

Susannah smiled reassuringly. "Go along—we'll be fine," she said.

"Hadn't ye best get to bed?" Nate asked Hannah.

"No. Remember that I'm no stranger to this—I've helped Mother bring many a babe into the world. 'Tis better for me to stay on my feet as long as I can."

"Take Gray Wolf with you," Susannah suggested as Nate

reached for his woolen cloak.

Looking relieved to be leaving, Gray Wolf followed Nate outside.

Susannah turned to Hannah with a smile. "This is one of those times when men just get in the way," she said.

Hannah nodded. "Poor Nate. I know he's worried about this birthing. He waited so long to marry and start a family—I pray I can give him a healthy son."

With a pang, Susannah thought of the baby she had lost. "If not this time, then another."

Hannah bit her lip and gripped Susannah's hand, but she shook her head when Susannah asked if another pain had seized her. "I know this must be hard for you," Hannah said. "Gray Wolf seems to be a good man, and he obviously cares for you very much. You two will have beautiful babies."

"If God wills it," Susannah said. "But right now, let's ask Him to help get your babe birthed."

❦

On their way to Lexington, Nate talked to Gray Wolf, partly to take his mind off Hannah's labor, but also because the white Indian interested him. If this strange man intended to marry his wife's cousin, it was Nate's duty as a representative of her family to make sure that he would be good to Susannah.

"'Tis a hard thing for a man to see his wife sufferin' to bring his child into the world," Nate said.

"I know about this," Gray Wolf said.

Nate looked at him in surprise. "You have children?"

"A son. He and his mother both dead."

Putting himself in Gray Wolf's place, Nate felt genuine compassion. "I'm sorry. Did she die in childbirth?"

"No. *Schwannack* killed them." Gray Wolf looked steadily at Nate. "Whites kill our people, we raid whites. It is not good."

Nate nodded in agreement. "For the sake of our children, we must learn to live in peace."

"It is a hard thing," Gray Wolf said.

"Yes, for us all it is hard. But it must be done."

"When I take seed corn to Black Oak's village, I will tell him you say this."

"Will Susannah go back with you?" Nate asked after a moment.

Gray Wolf nodded. "She is my woman," he said.

"Some would say she belongs here with her own people," Nate said.

"If Su-sannah want that, she stay here."

"Ye will not make her go back with ye against her will?" Nate probed.

Gray Wolf's mouth made a straight line. "I have said it."

Nate almost smiled. "Then I guess Hannah and I'll just have to pray for ye both."

❧

Mary Chandler welcomed Nate warmly and seemed amused by his agitation when he explained his errand.

"I'll send my bond-girl out to find the midwife whilst you and your friend take a bit of lunch wi' me," she said. "Now tell me who this young man is—I've not seen him in these parts."

Seeing no help for it, Nate reluctantly sat down to the hot food Mary offered, although he was so distracted he scarcely knew that he ate.

"This is Bill Gray," Nate said, using the name that Susannah had earlier suggested. "He and my wife's cousin Susannah are going to be wed."

"Susannah Campbell is *alive?*" Mary shrieked and clutched her throat. "Praise God! How does this come to be?"

"Bill here saved her from the river. He lives in the Indian Territory, where they plan to go after they're married. That's enough stew, thank ye—I've not much appetite this day."

Nate knew the story of Susannah's miraculous return from death would soon be all over Lexington. Gray Wolf listened, but made no objection to Nate's version of events, which was, after all, the truth.

"Well, I never!" exclaimed Mary Chandler. She threw her arms around Gray Wolf and hugged him fiercely. "You're getting a fine woman, sir. I hope I'll be invited to attend the nuptials."

Gray Wolf stared at her blankly, then looked to Nate for help.

"We don't yet know when the weddin' will be," Nate answered for him, "but I'm sure ye'll be welcome to come."

Mary slammed her hand down on the table so hard the trenchers jumped. "Why don't you have the weddin' right here, then? Reverend McAnnally has preached in this very room many a time—I reckon he'd not mind marryin' someone here, for a change."

"Thank ye kindly. I'll keep it in mind," Nate said.

Mary looked at Gray Wolf again. "He don't talk much, do he? But I reckon Susannah'll talk enough for them both. My, but I'll be glad to see her again."

Mary Chandler's bond-servant stuck her head into the room and nodded timidly at her visitors. "Miz Chandler?"

"Well, did you find Miz Perkins? Is she on her way?" Mary Chandler asked.

"Well'm, yes and no. I found her, but she's with Miz Meigs and she said to tell you she can't leave in the middle of a birthing. She will get to Miz McIntyre as soon as she can."

"How many children does Sally Meigs already have, Sally?" Mary Chandler asked.

The servant thought a moment, then held up three fingers. "If I don't mistake me, this 'un makes four."

"Well, then, don't look like that, Nate," Mary Chandler said jovially. "This babe shouldn't take but a little while, then Miz Perkins'll be on her way."

"I think we should wait for her at the Meigs' house," Nate said.

Mary Chandler looked disappointed. "I was hopin' to hear more about Susannah," she said. "Now don't forget about havin' the weddin' here," she said to Gray Wolf as they left.

"That woman has much talk," Gray Wolf said as they made their way to the Meigs' house, a few hundred yards away.

Nate nodded. "Aye, but she's a good soul, and ye and Susannah could do worse than to marry at her place. 'Twould be more convenient for Hannah—" As if reminded anew of his errand, Nate quickened his pace.

❧

Afterward, each had a different version of what actually happened that clear January day when Nathan Stone McIntyre entered the world. Nate claimed that the infant's first cry greeted him as he walked into the cabin with the midwife. However, Susannah, who had delivered the baby, and Hannah, his mother, both said that the boy was born several minutes before his father made it back from Lexington. The only one with no opinion in the matter was Gray Wolf, who had accepted Mary Chandler's invitation to stay in her lodgings until things settled down in the McIntyre household, and therefore wasn't there.

At any rate, Hannah seemed to suffer no ill effects from the lack of a midwife's services, and the baby, red-faced and with an almost insatiable appetite, could not be any healthier.

So well had everything gone that when young Nathan—they had agreed he would never be called "Nate"—was only three days old, they all went to Lexington, where Mary Chandler had made the arrangements for Bill Gray and Susannah McKay Campbell to be married at her house.

Susannah wore one of Hannah's dresses, and Mary Chandler added a square of lace that passed for a veil. Although Nate was far too tall and slender for most of his clothes to fit the sturdier-built Gray Wolf, he did have one fine lawn shirt that he brought him to put on at the last minute.

"I never see so many white people before," Gray Wolf told

Susannah when she reached Mary Chandler's house.

"Do you count yourself?" Susannah asked him, not expecting an answer. Gray Wolf seemed to be gradually accepting his white heritage, but she was fully aware that his willingness to marry her as "Bill Gray" did not necessarily mean that he felt comfortable about it.

"Reverend McAnnally say with God is no white or Indian," he said.

For the past two days he and Mr. McAnnally had had many conversations. Earlier that day, the reverend had told Susannah he was convinced that Gray Wolf had already received salvation.

"He does not yet understand all that it means to follow Christ, but ye can help him," Reverend McAnnally told her.

Susannah was happy over the news, but she also felt inadequate to provide Gray Wolf with spiritual guidance. "I am not sure I'll ever understand it all myself," she told him.

"Och, but ye know enough to ask for help, do ye not? Is it not your testimony that the Holy Spirit led you through what might have been certain death?"

"Yes, it is true," Susannah said.

"Never forget God, and all will be well with ye and your house," he had told her.

Now as they entered the Chandler house to loud greetings from the crowd of well-wishers who had already gathered there, the minister nodded to Nate. The crowd quieted as Nate picked up his fiddle and played the "Old Hundred" air. Then the minister took his place before the fireplace and opened the book from which he would read the wedding ceremony.

Susannah cast a sidewise glance at Gray Wolf as they bowed their heads for the opening prayer. The ritual was familiar to Susannah, but she knew that to Gray Wolf, it all must seem as foreign as the ceremony by which Black Oak had bound them had been to her.

Oh, Lord, make this mean as much to him as it means to me, she prayed.

When the time came for them to repeat the vows, Susannah faced Gray Wolf and smiled her encouragement.

"Do you, Bill Gray, take this woman—" the minister began.

"Bill Gray Wolf," Gray Wolf interrupted loudly. "It is my name."

The minister ignored the collective murmur that had greeted Gray Wolf's words and started again. "Do you, Bill Gray Wolf, take this woman to be your lawfully wedded wife?"

Susannah held her breath until Reverend McAnnally finished the question and she heard Gray Wolf's strong answer.

"I do," he said, as if he truly meant it.

When the ceremony ended and the couple had been pronounced man and wife, everyone gathered around, eager to be the first to kiss the bride and shake the groom's hand.

Nate McIntyre struck up a lively fiddle tune, and Mary Chandler and some of the other women brought out food for all the guests.

While the festivities were at their height, Nate signaled that it was time for them to leave. Amid a final chorus of shouted congratulations, Susannah and Gray Wolf ran outside, where their horse waited to take them back to the McIntyres'. Hannah and Nate and their baby would stay on with Mary Chandler for a few more days. When the McIntyres returned to their cabin, Susannah and Gray Wolf would travel back to Black Oak's village with the seed corn and other provisions they had purchased.

Susannah wrapped her arms tightly around her husband's waist, laid her head against his broad back, and realized that she had never been happier. *Dear God, thank You for this day,* she thought. She hoped that Gray Wolf felt the same way, but she did not try to ask him. For now, Susannah was content merely to be with Gray Wolf, who was, at last, her man forever.

When they reached the cabin, Gray Wolf walked the horse to the lean-to and lifted Susannah down before he bent to kiss her.

"White man's binding takes long time," he said when he finally let her go.

"It didn't hurt, though," Susannah said. "No cutting this time."

Gray Wolf held Susannah's wrist and traced the faint line at the place where their blood had mingled. "That mark always there," he said.

Susannah took his hand in both of hers and placed it first over her heart, then on his. "Our binding today is always here," she said.

"God knows this?" Gray Wolf asked, and Susannah nodded.

"Yes. God is the reason we are together. Do you believe this?"

Gray Wolf nodded. "Yes." He bent his head to kiss her again. "No more talk," he whispered.

This time, Susannah joyfully obeyed.

author's note

The McKay, Craighead, Stone, McIntyre, Campbell, and Graywolf families are all entirely fictional. However, thousands of pioneers like them braved the unknown to create the country whose freedom we enjoy today. In addition to stamina and courage, almost all of these men and women also possessed a deep and abiding faith in God. For historical information I am indebted to several sources, including the fine nonfiction books of Allan W. Eckert in general and his *The Frontiersmen* in particular. In addition, the microfilmed Draper Manuscript Collection provided many fascinating glimpses into the everyday lives of Trans-Allegheny pioneers who fought the terrain, wild animals, and Indians to claim and hold their own land.

Today, paved interstate highways measure in minutes travel that once took days. In the comfort of our homes, we may forget that several generations of our ancestors made do with drafty log cabins—hot in the summer, cold in the winter, and open to flies and other insects. We would not, of course, want to return to those times, but knowing what their lives were like can make us appreciate what we might otherwise take for granted.

If you're interested in learning more about the early times in your area, the public library is a wonderful place to begin. In addition, local, state, and regional historical societies continue to gather and preserve information about America's past for our own and future generations.

The "faith of our fathers" gave birth to and nourished America.

Our own faith must sustain it.

A Letter To Our Readers

Dear Reader:

In order that we might better contribute to your reading enjoyment, we would appreciate your taking a few minutes to respond to the following questions. When completed, please return to the following:

Rebecca Germany, Editor
Heartsong Presents
P.O. Box 719
Uhrichsville, Ohio 44683

1. Did you enjoy reading *Sign of the Spirit*?
   ❑ Very much. I would like to see more books
      by this author!
   ❑ Moderately
      I would have enjoyed it more if _____

   _____

2. Are you a member of *Heartsong Presents*? Yes   No
   If no, where did you purchase this book? _____

   _____

3. What influenced your decision to purchase this
   book? (Check those that apply.)

   ❑ Cover   ❑ Back cover copy

   ❑ Title   ❑ Friends

   ❑ Publicity   ❑ Other _____

4. **On a scale from 1 (poor) to 10 (superior), please rate the following elements.**

___Heroine   ___Plot

___Hero   ___Inspirational theme

___Setting   ___Secondary characters

5. **What settings would you like to see covered in *Heartsong Presents* books?**

_____

_____

6. **What are some inspirational themes you would like to see treated in future books?**_____

_____

_____

7. **Would you be interested in reading other *Heartsong Presents* titles?**   ❏ Yes   ❏ No

8. **Please check your age range:**
❏ Under 18   ❏ 18-24   ❏ 25-34
❏ 35-45   ❏ 46-55   ❏ Over 55

9. **How many hours per week do you read?** _____

Name _____

Occupation _____

Address _____

City _____ State_____ Zip _____

Hearts❤ng Presents
Love Stories Are Rated G!

That's for godly, gratifying, and of course, great! If you love a thrilling love story, but don't appreciate the sordidness of popular paperback romances, **Heartsong Presents** is for you. In fact, **Heartsong Presents** is the *only inspirational romance book club*, the only one featuring love stories where Christian faith is the primary ingredient in a marriage relationship.

Sign up today to receive your first set of four, never before published Christian romances. Send no money now; you will receive a bill with the first shipment. You may cancel at any time without obligation, and if you aren't completely satisfied with any selection, you may return the books for an immediate refund!

Imagine. . .four new romances every month—two historical, two contemporary—with men and women like you who long to meet the one God has chosen as the love of their lives. . .all for the low price of $9.97 postpaid.

To join, simply complete the coupon below and mail to the address provided. **Heartsong Presents** romances are rated G for another reason: They'll arrive *Godspeed!*

Luke watched her step from the car and disappear. He rushed out his door and ran to find her crumpled body on the driveway, her face looking shocked. "Are you okay?" he asked.

"I'll take that hand after all, Dr. Marcusson." As Luke lifted her from the concrete her warm scent filled his senses. He closed his eyes and allowed the moment to overwhelm him before he remembered that she was his patient. He had no business being at her home, but how could he have allowed her to go alone in a cab? He might have called his cousin Katie, her secretary, but that would have broken patient confidentiality.

Clearly, God had led him there and now he would have to be worthy of the call. He straightened and took a step back while still holding firmly onto her arms to help her balance. Walking backward, he led her up the steps to her wide front porch. Proverbs 31, where God describes a godly wife, suddenly popped into his mind, along with a new insight. A desirable woman that needed him was certainly more temptation than he was capable of handling alone. He remembered the verse about beauty being fleeting and now fully understood its meaning. This woman was truly captivating.

KRISTIN BILLERBECK lives in Northern California with her husband, an engineering director and their three small boys. A marketing director by profession, Kristin now stays home to be with her children and writes for enjoyment. This is her second inspirational novel.

Books by Kristin Billerbeck

HEARTSONG PRESENTS
HP247—Strong as the Redwood

Don't miss out on any of our super romances. Write to us at the following address for information on our newest releases and club information.

Heartsong Presents Readers' Service
PO Box 719
Uhrichsville, OH 44683